# CHAPTER ONE

CESARIO DI SILVESTRI could not sleep.

Events in recent months had brought him to a personal crossroads, at which he had acted with innate decisiveness: he had stripped the chaff from his life in order to focus his energy on what *really* mattered, only to appreciate that, while he had worked tirelessly to become an extraordinarily wealthy tycoon, he had put next to no work at all into his private life. The only close friend he fully trusted still was Stefano, the cousin he had grown up with. He'd had many women in his bed, but only one whom he'd loved—and he had treated her so carelessly that she had fallen in love with someone else. He was thirty-three years old and he had never even come close to marrying. What did that say about him?

Was he a natural loner or simply a commitment-phobe? He groaned out loud, exasperated by the constant flow of philosophical thoughts that had recently dogged him, because all his life, to date, he had been a doer rather than a thinker: a great sportsman, a dynamic and cold-blooded businessman. Giving up on sleep, Cesario pulled on some shorts and strode through his magnificent Moroccan villa, impervious to the opulent trappings of the billionaire's lifestyle that had lately come to mean so little to him. He filled a tumbler with ice cold water and drank it down thirstily.

As he had admitted to Stefano, by this age he would have liked to have had a child, only not with the kind of woman who cared more about money than anything else. For such a woman would only raise her child with the same shallow self-seeking values.

'But it's not too late for you to start a family,' Stefano had declared with conviction. 'Nothing is set in stone, Cesario. Do what you *want*, not as you think you should.'

Hearing the shrill of his cell phone, Cesario headed back upstairs, wondering which of his staff thought it necessary to call him in the middle of the night. But there was nothing frivolous about that call from Rigo Castello, his security chief. Rigo was phoning to tell

## "I'm only going to kiss you," he imparted silkily.

Jess froze, her silvery eyes flickering with dismay at even that prospect. "No—"

"We have to start somewhere, *piccola mia*. There are some things I'm very good at," Cesario delivered with innate assurance. "And this is one of them."

And his mouth slid across her sealed-shut lips. She had expected passion, but he defied her expectations, and her heart set up an even louder thump behind her breastbone, the pace speeding up as he brushed his knowing mouth back over hers and the extent of her tension made her rigid. The tip of his tongue scored that seam of denial and her body came alive when she was least prepared for it, a jerky quiver of feminine response slivering through her with almost painful effect as she parted her lips to let him kiss her properly.

"That's enough," she said shakily, her hands rising against his broad shoulders to push him back from her.

"No, it's only the beginning," Cesario husked, smoldering golden eyes roving boldly over her averted face.

"This wedding you mentioned," Jess remarked hurriedly, "When would it take place?"

"As soon as it can be arranged—it *will* be a proper wedding," Cesario decreed without hesitation. "With the dress, the big guest list, the whole bridal show."

"Why did you choose me for this?" she heard herself ask without warning.

His dense lashes swooped low over his brilliant dark gaze. "Ask me on our wedding night," he advised, a piece of advice which not unnaturally silenced her. …

**SECRETLY PREGNANT...
CONVENIENTLY WED!**

*With this ring, I claim my baby!*

The amazing new trilogy by
bestselling Harlequin Presents® author

# Lynne Graham

The charming and pretty English village of
Charlbury St. Helens is home to three young
women whose Cinderella lives are about to be
turned upside down...by three of the wealthiest,
most handsome and impossibly
arrogant men in Europe!

Jemima, Flora and Jess aren't looking for love,
but all have babies very much in mind. Jemima
already has a young son, Flora is hoping to adopt
her late half sister's little daughter,
and Jess just longs to be a mum.

But whether they have or want a baby, all the girls
must marry ultimate alpha males to keep their
dreams.... And Alejandro, Angelo and Cesario are
not about to be tamed!

SECRETLY PREGNANT...CONVENIENTLY WED!

*Jemima's Secret—March
Flora's Defiance—April
Jess's Promise—May*

# Lynne Graham

## JESS'S PROMISE

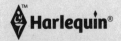

TORONTO NEW YORK LONDON
AMSTERDAM PARIS SYDNEY HAMBURG
STOCKHOLM ATHENS TOKYO MILAN MADRID
PRAGUE WARSAW BUDAPEST AUCKLAND

Recycling programs
for this product may
not exist in your area.

ISBN-13: 978-0-373-23751-7

JESS'S PROMISE

First North American Publication 2011

Copyright © 2011 by Lynne Graham

This edition published by arrangement with Harlequin Books S.A.

For questions and comments about the quality of this book
please contact us at Customer_eCare@Harlequin.ca.

www.eHarlequin.com

**Printed in U.S.A.**

# JESS'S PROMISE

him that he'd just been robbed: a painting, a recent acquisition worth a cool half-million pounds, had been stolen from Halston Hall, his English country home, and apparently the theft had been an inside job. Cold outrage swept Cesario at that concluding fact. He didn't get mad, he got even. He paid his employees handsomely and treated them well and in return he expected loyalty. When the guilty party was finally identified, Cesario would ensure that the full weight of the law was brought to bear on him…

But, within a few minutes, his outrage and annoyance subsided to a bearable level and a grim smile began to tug at his handsome mouth as he contemplated his now inevitable visit to his beautiful Elizabethan home in England. There he would undoubtedly run into his very beautiful Madonna of the stable yard again, as his horses required her regular attention. And unlike the many women he had known and deemed to be almost interchangeable, his English Madonna did rejoice in one unique quality: she was the only woman who had ever said no to Cesario di Silvestri…and utterly infuriated and frustrated him. One dinner date and he'd been history, rejected out of hand by a woman for the first time in his life and he still had no idea why. For Cesario, who was by nature fiercely competitive, she would always be a mystery and a challenge...

A small, slightly built brunette with her long dark curly hair caught up in a practical ponytail, Jess kept up a constant stream of soothing chatter while she wielded the shears over the cowering dog's matted coat.

The job had to be done. As the sheepdog's painfully emaciated body was revealed Jess's soft full mouth hardened; the suffering of animals always upset her and she had trained as a veterinary surgeon in an effort to do what she could to help in the way of welfare.

Her volunteer helper at weekends, a pretty blonde schoolgirl, helped to keep the dog steady. 'How is he?' Kylie asked with concern.

Jess sent the teenager a wry look. 'Not bad for his age. He's an old dog. He'll be fine once I've seen to his sores and fed him up a bit.'

'But the older ones are very hard to rehome.' Kylie sighed.

'You never know,' Jess said with determined optimism, though actually she did know very well. The little tribe of dogs she had personally rescued in recent years were a motley group, each of which was either older, maimed or suffering from behavioural problems. Few people were willing to take a chance on such dogs.

When Jess had embarked on her first job in the village of Charlbury St Helens, she had lived above the vet's surgery where she worked. But she'd had to find other accommodation when the practice's senior partner had decided to expand the business and turned the small flat into an office suite instead. Jess had been lucky enough to find a run-down cottage with a collection of old sheds to rent just outside the village. Although her home was not much to look at and offered only basic comforts, it came with two fields and the landlord had agreed to her opening a small animal sanctuary there. Even though she earned a good salary she was always broke, because every penny she could spare went towards animal feed and medical supplies. Even so, in doing what she loved, she was happier than she had ever been in her life. But then she would be the first to admit that she had long preferred animals to people. Shy, socially awkward and uneasy with men after a traumatic experience at university that had left her with both physical and mental scars, Jess struggled to fit in with human beings but was totally at home with four-legged beasts.

The sound of a car pulling up outside sent Kylie to the door of the shed. 'It's your dad, Jess.'

Jess glanced up in surprise; Robert Martin rarely called in on her at weekends. Recently, in fact, she had seen less than usual of her father and, when she had, he had seemed abnormally preoccupied with work. As a rule, though, he was a regular visitor, who often helped out by repairing the animal housing and the fences. A quiet man in his fifties, he was a good husband and an even better dad, for, while other family members had believed that Jess had been aiming too high in dreaming of becoming a veterinary surgeon, Robert had encouraged his daughter's dream every step of the way. His love and support meant all the more to Jess when she reflected that while Robert was the only father she had ever known he had had nothing whatsoever to do with her conception. That, however, was a secret known to few outside the family circle.

'I'll get on with the feeding,' Kylie proffered, as the stocky grey-haired older man nodded to her and entered the shed.

'I'll be with you in a minute, Dad,' Jess promised, bending over the prone dog to attend to his wounds with antiseptic ointment. 'It's not like you to call in on a Sunday morning…'

'I need to talk to you. You'll be at church later and you're often on duty in the evening at weekends,' he said gruffly, and something odd in his voice made her lift her head, her unusually light grey eyes questioning.

She frowned because the older man looked pale and strained and every year of his age and more. 'What's happened?' she prompted in dismay. She had not seen him look that frightened since her mother's diagnosis of cancer the previous year.

'Finish up with your patient first.'

With difficulty Jess mastered the spasm of fear that had immediately rippled through her. Goodness, had her mother's cancer returned? That was her first panicky thought and her hands shook slightly as she finished her task. As far as she was aware, though, her mother had not had a check-up scheduled and she told herself off for being so quick to expect bad news. 'Go into the house and wait for me. I won't be long,' she told him briskly, suppressing her apprehension.

She put the dog into a pen where food was already waiting for him and briefly watched the animal tuck into what was obviously his first proper meal in weeks. After pausing in the bathroom to scrub her hands clean, she hurried on into the house and then the kitchen where Robert Martin had already seated himself at the worn pine table.

'What's wrong?' she prompted tautly, too anxious where her mother was concerned even to put her fear into words.

Her father looked up, his brown eyes full of guilt and anxiety. 'I've done something stupid, really *really* stupid. I'm sorry to bring it to your doorstep but I can't face telling your mother yet,' he confided tightly. 'She's been through so much lately but I'm afraid that this business will break her...'

'Just spit it out...tell me what's happened,' Jess pressed gently, sitting down opposite him, convinced he had to be innocently exaggerating his predicament because she just could not imagine him doing anything seriously wrong. He was a plain-spoken man of moderate habits, well liked and respected in the neighbourhood. 'What did you do that was so stupid?'

Robert Martin shook his greying head heavily. 'Well, to start with, I borrowed a lot of money and from the wrong people…'

His daughter's eyes opened very wide, for his explanation had taken her aback. 'Money is the problem? You've got into debt?'

The older man gave a weary sigh. 'That was only the beginning. Do you remember that holiday I took your mother on after her treatment?'

Jess nodded slowly. Her father had swept her mother off on a cruise that had been the holiday of a lifetime for a couple who had never earned enough to take such breaks away from home before. 'I *was* surprised that you could afford it, but you said that the money came from your savings.'

Shamed by that reminder, Robert shook his head dully 'I lied. There were never any savings. I never managed to put any money aside in the way I'd hoped when I was younger. Things have always been tight for us as a family.'

'So you must have borrowed the money for that cruise—who did you borrow from?'

'Your mother's brother, Sam Welch,' Robert

admitted reluctantly, watching his daughter's face tighten in consternation.

'But Sam's a *loan shark*—you know he is! Mum's family are a bad lot and I've even heard you warn other people not to get mixed up with them,' Jess reminded him feelingly. 'Knowing what you do about Sam, how on earth could you have borrowed from him?'

'The bank turned me down flat when I approached them. Your uncle Sam was my only option and, because he was sorry your mother had been ill, he said he'd wait for the loan to be repaid. He was very nice, very reasonable. But now his sons have taken over his business, and Jason and Mark have a very different attitude to the people who owe them money.'

Jess groaned out loud and she was already wondering frantically how she could possibly help when she had no savings of her own. That realisation made her feel very guilty, since she earned more than either her parents or her two younger brothers, yet she was still not in a position to offer assistance. But, perhaps, she thought frantically, *she* might be able to take out a loan.

'The original amount I borrowed has grown and grown with the interest charges.

And Jason and Mark have been at me almost every day for months now,' the older man told her heavily. 'Coming after me in the car when I was out working, phoning me at all times of the day and night, constantly reminding me how much I owe them. It's been a nightmare keeping this wretched business from your mother. Jason and Mark wore me down—I was desperate to get them off my back! I had no hope of paying that money back any time soon, so when they offered me a deal—'

Jess gave him a bewildered look and cut in, 'A deal? What kind of a deal?'

'I was a bloody fool, but they said they'd write off what I owed if I helped them out.'

The look of overwhelming fear and regret in her father's face was making Jess so tense that she felt nauseous. 'What on earth did you help them to do?'

'They told me they wanted to take pictures of the inside of Halston Hall and sell them to one of those celebrity magazines…you know, the sort of thing your mother reads,' Robert extended with all the vagueness of a man who had never even bothered to look through such a publication. 'You know how Jason has always boasted that he's a really good photographer and Mark said the photos would be worth a small fortune. I didn't see any real harm in it.'

'You didn't see any harm in it?' Jess repeated incredulously. 'Letting strangers go into your employer's home?'

'I won't pretend that I didn't know that Mr di Silvestri wouldn't like it. I know how he is about his privacy. Of course I do,' her father admitted unhappily. 'But I also thought— wrongly—that there was no way anyone would ever find out that I'd been responsible for letting Jason and Mark into the house, or even that it was them who had got in.'

True comprehension finally slotted into place and Jess was impelled up out of her chair, a look of horror stamping her finely moulded features. 'Oh, my goodness, the break-in at the hall…the painting that was stolen! Were you involved in the robbery?' she demanded in ringing disbelief. 'Was it your fault it happened?'

'That same evening I gave Jason and Mark my security access codes and key card for the house,' Robert admitted shakily, his complexion the colour of grey clay as he stared pleadingly at her. 'I honestly believed that it was only photos they wanted, Jess. I had no idea they were going to steal anything, but I suspect now that it was all planned and I was an idiot to swallow the story they fed me.'

'You have to go to the police right now and tell them what you know!' Jess exclaimed.

'I won't need to…the police will be coming for me very soon,' Robert countered in a bleak rejoinder. 'I found out last night that Mr di Silvestri's security system is so sophisticated that the IT consultant he's bringing in will be able to tell which employee's access code was used to gain entry to the hall and switch off the alarm. Apparently we all have individual codes, so the boss will know soon enough that it was me.'

Chilled to the bone by that news, Jess suppressed a shiver. She was appalled; there was no point pretending otherwise. Her cousins, Jason and Mark Welch, had undoubtedly set her father up to gain access to the hall. They had deliberately subjected him to continual threatening visitations about the debt he could not repay, before finally approaching him with their seemingly simple little proposition. The older man had been naïve indeed to swallow their story of only wanting to take photographs. But then he *was* naïve, Jess conceded painfully; an uneducated handyman on the Halston estate, who until that cruise had never travelled more than fifty miles from his birthplace or worked in any other environment.

'Did the Welchs steal the painting?'

'I know nothing about what happened that night. I just handed over the codes and the key card, which was put back through the letterbox before I even got up the next morning,' he admitted heavily. 'The week after, Jason and Mark warned me to keep my mouth shut. Later, when I spoke to them about the robbery, they insisted that they had had nothing to do with it and that they have an alibi for that evening. I'm not sure I can see them as international art thieves. I wonder if they gave the codes and card to someone else to use. But I really haven't a clue.'

Jess was thinking sickly about Cesario di Silvestri, the billionaire Italian industrialist, the theft of whose painting her father would ultimately be held responsible for. Not a man to take such a crime lying down, not the forgiving sort either. How many people would even credit her father's version of events? Or that he had not willingly conspired with his wife's cousins? The fact that he had worked for almost forty years for the Halston estate would cut no ice, any more than his current lack of a criminal record and his good reputation. The bottom line was that a very serious offence had been committed.

As the older man took his leave and urged her not to mention the matter to her mother yet Jess frowned in disagreement. 'You need to tell Mum about this and quickly,' she objected. 'It'll be a much bigger shock for her if the police turn up and she doesn't know.'

'Stress could make her ill again,' Robert argued worriedly.

'You don't know that. Whatever happens, there are no guarantees,' Jess reminded her father of the oncologist's wise words following her mother's treatment programme the previous year. 'We just have to pray and hope for the best.'

'I've let her down…' Robert shook his head slowly, his dark eyes filmed with tears. 'She doesn't deserve this.'

Jess said nothing, as she had no words of comfort to offer; the future did indeed look bleak. Should she approach Cesario di Silvestri and speak up on her father's behalf? Unfortunately, when she thought about the background to her own distinctly awkward relationship with Cesario di Silvestri, that did not seem quite such a bright idea. She had gone out to dinner with Cesario once. When he had invited her, she'd had no choice but to accept out of courtesy, because of her father's employment with him, and also because he was their most important client at the practice. Her face still burned though whenever she thought back to that disastrous evening when everything that could have gone wrong had done so. Now, she hated visiting the Halston Hall stud while Cesario was in residence. He always made her feel horribly self-conscious and her professional confidence took a nose-dive around him.

Not that he was rude to her; in fact, she had never met anyone with more polished manners. She could not accuse the smoothly spoken Italian of harassment either, because he had never made the smallest attempt to ask her out again since. But there was always an ironic edge to his attitude that made her feel uncomfortable, as though she was a figure of fun in his eyes. She had never understood why he'd invited her out in the first place. After all, she bore no resemblance to the ex-tremely decorative and flirtatious party girls, socialites and starlets who usually entertained him.

Cesario di Silvestri had a downright notorious

reputation with the female sex, and Jess was very well aware of the fact. After all, her parents lived next door to his former housekeeper, Dot Smithers. The stories Dot had told of wild house parties and loose women flown in for the benefit of the rich male guests were the staples of village legend and had provided the fodder for several sleazy tabloid spreads in the years since the Italian billionaire had bought the Halston Hall estate. More than once Jess had personally seen Cesario di Silvestri with two or more women vying for his attention and she had no reason to doubt the rumour that he did, on occasion, enjoy more than one woman at a time in his bed.

So, in the light of that information, there had never been any question of Jess wanting an invitation to dine out or in with Cesario. Even without all the attendant scandal of his raunchy lifestyle, she remained convinced that he was way out of her league, both in looks and status, and she very firmly believed that nothing good could develop from a relationship based on such obvious inequality. In her opinion, people from different walks of life should respect the boundaries that kept them separate. Her own mother, after all, had paid a high price when she'd chosen to flout those boundaries as a teenager.

And Jess's belief in that social division had only been underlined by that catastrophic dinner date. Cesario had taken her to an exclusive little restaurant and she had quickly realised she was seriously underdressed in comparison with the other female diners. He'd had to translate the stupid pretentious menu written in a foreign language for her benefit. During the meal she had struggled in sinking mortification to understand which pieces of cutlery went with which course and was still covered in blushes at the recollection that she had eaten her dessert with a spoon rather than the fork Cesario had used.

But the highlight of the evening had to have been his invitation for her to spend the night with him after just one kiss. Cesario di Silvestri wasn't just fast with women, he was supersonic. But his move on her had outraged her pride and hurt her self-image. Had she struck him as being so cheap and easy that she would fall into bed with a man she barely knew?

All right, so the kiss had been spectacular. But the dizzy sexuality he had engulfed her in with his practised technique had unnerved

her and had only made her all the more determined not to repeat such a dangerous experience. She had far too much self-respect and
common sense to plunge into an affair with
an impossibly wealthy womaniser. Such an
imbalanced relationship could lead to nothing
but grief, the results of which she had already
seen within her own family circle. In all likelihood, if she had slept with Cesario that night
he would have ticked some obnoxious male
mental score-sheet and never have asked her
out again.

In any case, in recent years Jess had pretty
much given up dating in favour of a quiet un-
complicated existence. Her sole regret on that
issue was that she adored children and, from
her teenage years, had dreamt of one day becoming a mother and having a child of her
own. Now, with her thirty-first birthday only
months away, she was afraid that she might
never have a baby and she made the most of
enjoying her brother's two young children.
She also recognised that in many ways her
pets took the place of offspring in her affec-
tions. Once or twice she had considered the
option of conceiving and raising a child alone,
only to shrink from the stressful challenge of
becoming a single parent who already worked

long unsocial hours. Children were also supposed to do best with a father figure in their lives and in such a scenario she would not be able to offer that possibility; she did not think it would be fair to burden her own father with such an expectation.

The following morning, after a disturbed night of sleep, Jess went into the surgery, where she checked on the sole resident patient, a cat with liver disease. After carrying out routine tasks, she took care of the emergency clinic, which encompassed everything from a goldfish in a bowl that was as dead as a doornail, to a dog she had to muzzle to treat and a moulting but healthy parrot.

That night she lay awake worrying about her father until almost dawn. Her mother, Sharon, had not phoned, which she knew meant that Robert had not yet summoned up the courage to tell his wife that he was in trouble. Jess's heart bled at the prospect of her mother's pain and anxiety once she understood the situation. Mother and daughter had always been very close.

Jess had little hope that a personal appeal to Cesario di Silvestri would help her father's cause. After all, why would anything *she* had to say carry any influence with him? On the other hand, if there was even the smallest chance that she *could* make a difference she knew she owed it to her family to at least *try*. Already painfully aware that Cesario had arrived the previous evening in the UK, she accepted that she needed to make her approach to him as soon as possible.

On Tuesday she was scheduled to make a regular check on the brood mares at the Halston stud and she planned to make her move then. With her travelled half of her little tribe of dogs, for she routinely divided them into two groups and took one out with her on alternate days. Today there was Johnson, a collie with three legs and one eye after a nasty accident with farm machinery, Dozy, a former racing greyhound who suffered from narcolepsy and fell sleep everywhere she went, and Hugs, a giant wolfhound, who became excessively anxious when Jess vanished from his view.

Cesario knew Jessica Martin was on his land the instant he saw the three scruffy dogs outside the archway that led into the big stable yard. He smiled at the familiar sight, while idly wondering why she burdened herself with other people's rejects; a less appealing collection of misfits would have been hard to find. The tatty hound was whining and fussing like an overgrown, fractious toddler, the greyhound was fast asleep in a puddle, while the collie was plastered fearfully against the wall, shrinking in terror from the noise of a car that was nowhere near him.

As his head groom, Perkins, hurried to greet him, Cesario glanced straight past the middle aged man to rest his dark, deep-set gaze intently on the slight figure of the woman engaged in rifling her veterinary bag for a vaccination shot. A glimpse of the sheer classic purity of Jessica Martin's profile gave Cesario as much pleasure as the image of a Madonna in a fine Renaissance painting. Blessed with skin as rich and fine in texture as whipped cream, she had delicate but strong features and a luscious Cupid's-bow mouth worthy of a starring role in any red-blooded male's fantasies. And the footnote to that list of attributes was amazing eyes that were a luminous pale grey, as bright as silver in certain lights, and a foaming torrent of long black curly hair that she always kept tied back. She never used cosmetics or indeed wore anything the slightest bit feminine if she could help it, yet no matter how she dressed her diminutive height, beautiful bone structure and slender and subtle curves gave her an exceptionally arresting appearance.

Clad in faded riding breeches, workman-like boots and a waxed jacket that should have been thrown out years ago, she was the living, breathing antithesis of Cesario's usual taste in women. Cesario had always been a perfectionist and great wealth and success had only increased that natural inclination. He liked his women sophisticated, exquisitely groomed and clothed. Every time he saw Jess Martin he reminded himself of those facts and questioned the depth of her apparent appeal for him. Was it simply because she had once said no and sentenced him to a cold shower rather than the pleasure of slaking their mutual attraction? For, although she denied it and did what she could to hide the fact, the attraction *was* mutual. He had known it when she looked at him over the dinner table and, since then, every time she went out of her way to avoid his eyes or keep him at arm's length. Either some man had done a very good job of souring her attitude to his sex or she had a problem with intimacy.

But his suspicions about her had not the smallest cooling effect on him while those breeches clung to every line of her slender toned thighs and the gloriously pert swell of her behind. Strip off the clothes and she would be pure perfection. As the familiar stirring heaviness at his groin afflicted him, Cesario's perfect white teeth gritted behind his firmly modelled mouth. *Per l'amor di Dio!* He went from enjoying the view to exasperation because he had never been a guy happy to look without the right to touch. Lust from afar was not his style. She was not at all his type, he reminded himself brutally, recalling the dinner engagement from hell when she had turned up wearing a black tent dress and had barely talked. She didn't even know how to speak to him. Look at her now, pretending that she hadn't yet noticed him to put off the moment of having to acknowledge him for as long as she possibly could!

Jess felt almost paralysed by the awareness that Cesario di Silvestri was nearby. Prior to his arrival she had noted the frantic activities of the stable staff, keen to ensure that everything looked good for the boss's visit, and she could scarcely have missed the throaty roar of his Ferrari, for, while other men might have chosen a four-wheel drive to negotiate the rough estate roads, Cesario travelled everywhere in a jaw-droppingly expensive sports car. Slowly she turned her head and looked at him while he spoke to Donald Perkins and, in that split second of freedom, she took in her fill and more.

Cesario was so gorgeous that, even after a couple of years' exposure to him, his charismatic good looks still exercised a weird kind of fascination over Jess. With the exception of a tiny scar on his temple he was without flaw, an acknowledgement that only reminded her of her own physical scars, and which chilled her. Cesario stood comfortably over six feet tall and enjoyed the long, lean, powerful build of an athlete. Even in country casuals he looked as elegant as though he had just stepped off a fashion catwalk, as his garments were tailored to a perfect fit, enhancing his broad shoulders, narrow hips and long muscular thighs. He wore his black hair short and cropped and his skin carried the golden hue of the Mediterranean sun. His narrow-bridged arrogant nose, sleek, proud cheekbones and sardonic, sensual mouth were arranged in such a way that you looked at him and then immediately had to look back again. Turning back to her task, she wondered frantically what she was going to say to him about her father. The fact that Robert was still walking around free meant that the older man's role in the robbery had yet to be identified.

'Jessica...' Cesario murmured smoothly, refusing to accept being ignored.

Flustered, her cheeks warming with colour, for he was the only person alive who ignored the diminutive by which she was known and continually employed her baptismal name, Jess twisted back to him. 'Mr di Silvestri...'

Cesario was reluctantly impressed that she had finally pronounced his name correctly without stumbling over the syllables like a drunk. She'd simply ignored repeated invitations to call him by his first name, keeping him at a distance with her cool reserve. Then Perkins asked her advice about a stallion with a tendon injury that was not responding well to ice packs and bandaging and she accompanied him into the stables to examine the horse. Soldier was a valuable animal and the head groom should have called her in sooner to administer anti-inflammatory drugs, but Jess could not bring herself to criticise his decision to hold fire in front of his employer.

'Jessica should have been consulted the day the injury occurred,' Cesario commented, picking up on the oversight with ease.

Jess finished her tasks and moved slowly

towards the arch that led out of the courtyard. Sadly when, for once, she would have welcomed an attempt, Cesario made no move to keep her longer by striking up a conversation. Finally steeling herself, with her backbone rigid, she turned back and said without any expression at all and a tightness in the foot of her throat that gave her voice a husky edge, 'I'd appreciate a word with you, Cesario…'

Cesario settled brilliant dark eyes on her, making no attempt to hide his surprise at her use of his first name. Colour crept into her cheeks again as she gripped her bag between clenched fingers, fiercely uncomfortable below his intent scrutiny. Of course he was staring, one satiric ebony brow slightly quirked like a question mark because he could not imagine what she wanted. After all, she rarely spoke to him if she could help it.

'I'll be with you in a moment,' he responded in his rich, dark, accented drawl.

And no moment had ever stretched longer for Jess as she hovered with her dogs beyond the archway waiting for him. Worst of all she still had no idea at all of what she was planning to say to him…

# CHAPTER TWO

'PERHAPS we could conduct this dialogue over dinner this evening,' Cesario suggested with rich satisfaction.

The suggestion that she might be fishing for the chance to go out with him again inflamed Jess and stung her pride. She flipped round to face him, light grey eyes bright as silver with antagonism. 'No, I'm sorry, that wouldn't be appropriate. I need to talk to you about something relating to my family.'

'Your...*family*?' Lean dark features stamped with a bemused frown, Cesario dealt her an enquiring glance, contriving without effort to look so breathtakingly handsome that he momentarily made it virtually impossible for her to concentrate.

A prickling shimmy of sensation pinched her nipples to tautness and made her spine stiffen defensively, for she recognised that physical response for what it was and loathed it. He was a devastatingly handsome man and she was convinced that no healthy woman with hormones could be fully indifferent to that level of masculine magnetism. Her body was literally programmed to react in what she had long since mentally labelled a 'knee-jerk response' to Cesario's chemical appeal. It was Mother Nature, whose sexual conditioning she could not totally suppress, having the last laugh on her.

Her colour fluctuating in response to her rattled composure, Jess sent her eyes in a meaningful sweep in the direction of the stable staff still within hearing. 'I'd prefer not to discuss the matter out here.'

His attention locked onto her taut facial muscles and the nervous pulse flickering in a hollow at the base of her slender throat, Cesario was even more curious to find out what she could possibly be so wired up about. He was also noting in a haze of innate sensuality that her skin was so fine that he could see the faint blue tracery of her veins beneath it. That fast he wanted to see her naked, all that creamy skin bare and unadorned for his benefit. Naked and *willing*, he thought hungrily. 'Follow me up to the house, then,' he instructed, irritably shaking free of the sexual spell she could cast to swing into his low-slung sports car.

In the driving mirror he watched her coax the sleeping greyhound from the puddle up into her arms, without worrying about the mess the bedraggled animal would make of her clothes. As she settled the dog into the rear of the old Land Rover she drove her other pets fawned on her as if she had been absent a day rather than an hour. Aware she took in the local homeless animals, he had always been grudgingly impressed by her compassionate nature, even if he could not approve of her indifference to her appearance. Although she was beautiful she did not behave as if she was, and that could only intrigue a man accustomed to finding women superficial and predictable. Somewhere along the line something had happened to Jess Martin that had prevented her from developing the narcissistic outlook of a beauty and the expectation that she should always be the centre of attention.

Jess parked beside the Ferrari at the front of the magnificent rambling Elizabethan house. Built of mellow brick and ornamented by tall elaborate chimneys and rows of symmetrical mullioned windows that reflected the sunshine, Halston Hall had considerable charm and antiquity. Although Dot Smithers had on one memorable occasion entertained Jess and her mother in the kitchen quarters there, Jess had never set foot in the main house. The Dunn-Montgomery family, who had owned the hall for several centuries, and whose male heirs had been often prominent in government, had not held open days at their ancestral home. Dwindling cash resources had forced the family to sell up six years earlier. To the great relief of the staff, who had feared that the property would be broken up and that they would lose their jobs, Cesario di Silvestri had bought the estate in its entirety. He had renovated the house, rescued the failing land with modern farming methods and set up a very successful stud farm.

Dot's male replacement, following her early retirement, a middle-aged and rotund Italian known as Tommaso, ushered Jess indoors. The splendid hall was dominated by a massive Tudor chimney piece with a seventeenth-century date swirled in the plaster above it. Her nervous tension at an all-time high in the face of such grandeur, Jess defied the urge to satisfy her curiosity and gape at her surroundings. She was shown into a room fitted out

like a modern office, in surrealistic contrast
to the linen fold panelling on the walls and
the picturesque view of an ornate box-bush-
edged knot garden beyond the windows.

'Your family?' Cesario prompted with a
slight warning hint of impatience. Propped
up against the edge of what appeared to be
his desk in an attitude of relaxation, he was
the very epitome of English country-casual
style with a twist of elegant designer Italian in
his tailored open-necked shirt and beautifully
cut trousers.

'They're tenants of yours in the village, and
my father and my brothers work for you here
on the estate,' Jess volunteered.

'I was aware of those facts,' Cesario countered with a wry smile. 'My estate manager
made the connection for me the first time I
met you.'

Jess lifted her chin and straightened her
slight shoulders, wondering if that information had originally been given to emphasise
that she hailed from working-class country
stock, rather than the snobbish county set. If
so, the news of her humble beginnings and
lower social standing must have failed to dim
his initial interest, for the dinner invitation
had followed soon afterwards. Stubbornly

refusing to meet those gorgeous dark eyes in a head-on collision and blocking her awareness to him as she had learnt to do to maintain her composure and show of indifference, she breathed in deep. 'I have something to tell you and it relates to the robbery here…'

With a sudden flashing frown, Cesario leant forward, any hint of relaxation instantly banished by her opening words. 'The theft of my painting?'

Beneath that daunting stare, the colour in her cheeks steadily drained away. 'I'm afraid so.'

'If you have information relating to the robbery, why haven't you gone to the police with it?'

Jess could feel her ever-rising tension turning her skin clammy with nervous perspiration. Suddenly aware that she was way too warm, she shrugged free of the heavy jacket she wore over her shirt and draped it clumsily over the seat of the chair beside her. 'Because my father's involved and I was keen to get the chance to speak to you first.'

Cesario was not slow to grasp essential facts and his keen gaze glimmered as he instantly added two and two. As the estate handyman, who also acted as caretaker when the hall was unoccupied, Robert Martin had long been entrusted with the right to enter the hall at any time to perform maintenance checks and carry out repairs. 'If your father helped the thieves, you're wasting your time looking to me for sympathy—'

'Let me explain what happened first. I only found out about this matter yesterday. Last year my mother was diagnosed with breast cancer and it was a very stressful time for my family,' Jess told him tightly.

'While I am naturally sympathetic to anyone in your mother's situation, I fail to see what her ill health has to do with me or the loss of my painting,' Cesario asserted drily.

'If you listen, I'll tell you—'

'No. I think I am much more inclined in this scenario to call in the police and leave them to ask the questions. It's their job, not mine,' Cesario cut across her to declare with derision, his lean, darkly handsome features forbidding as he straightened and began to reach for the phone with a lean, shapely hand. 'I am not comfortable with this conversation.'

'Please don't phone the police yet!' Jess exclaimed, grey eyes wide with urgency as she moved forward suddenly, appearing as if she was trying to physically impose her slight body between him and the telephone. 'Please give me the chance to explain things first.'

'Get on with the explanation, then,' Cesario advised curtly, leaving the phone untouched, while surveying her with dark eyes flaming bronze with suspicion and anger. Even so, on a primitive masculine level he was already starting to get a kick out of her pleading with him. The tables had been turned with a vengeance, he savoured with satisfaction. She was no longer treating him to frozen silence or looking down that superior little nose of hers at him.

'Dad was worried sick about Mum and he wanted to take her away for a holiday after she finished her treatment, but he had to borrow the money to do so. Unfortunately he borrowed it from my uncle at an extortionate rate of interest.' Stumbling in her eagerness to tell the whole story, Jess outlined her father's efforts to deal with being pressed for his debt, followed by the approach and the offer made by her cousins.

'This is your *family* you're talking about,' Cesario reminded her dulcetly, marvelling at what she was willing to tell him about her less than scrupulous relations. For the first time it genuinely struck him that, for all her educational achievements, she truly was, unlike him, from the other side of the tracks.

'My mother's brother was in and out of prison for much of his life. He doesn't much care how he makes his money as long as he makes it. But his sons have never been in serious trouble with the police.' Her cheeks burned red with embarrassment as she filled in the disagreeable facts. 'My father believed what he was told—that Jason and Mark only wanted to get into this house to take photos which they could sell.'

Cesario dealt her a withering appraisal. 'This property is full of valuable antiques and art works. Are you seriously expecting me to believe that any man could be that stupid?'

'I don't think my father's stupid, I think he was simply desperate to do what they asked and be free of that debt. He was frantically trying to protect Mum from the distress of finding out how foolish he had been,' Jess confided ruefully. 'I don't believe he thought beyond that and what he did was very wrong. I'm not trying to excuse his behaviour. He's had access to this house for many years because he was a trusted employee and in acting as he did he betrayed your trust, but

I'm convinced that my cousins intentionally targeted him.'

His handsome mouth taut with angry constraint, Cesario studied her grimly. 'It is immaterial to me whether your father was deliberately set-up or otherwise. Your mother's illness, the debt that ensued...those are not my concerns. My sole interest is in the loss of my painting and unless you have information to offer about how it might be recovered and from whom...'

'I'm afraid that I don't know anything about that and nor, unfortunately, does my father. His only function that evening was handing over his key card and the codes for the alarm.'

'Which makes him as guilty as any man who conspires with thieves and provides them with the means of entry to private property,' Cesario pronounced without hesitation.

'He honestly didn't know that anything was going to be stolen! He's an honest man, not a thief.'

'An honest man would not have allowed the men you described into my home to do as they liked,' Cesario derided. 'Why did you make this approach to me? What response did you expect from me?'

'I hoped that you would accept that Dad was entirely innocent of the knowledge that a crime was being planned.'

His sardonic mouth curled. 'I have only your word for that. After all, there was a robbery and it would not have happened had your father proved worthy of the responsibility he'd been given.'

'Look, please listen to me,' she urged with passionate vehemence, her pale grey eyes insistent. 'He's not a bad man, he's not dishonest either, and he's devastated by the loss that his foolishness caused you—'

'Foolishness is far too kind a description of what I regard as a gross betrayal of trust,' Cesario interrupted in flat dismissal of her argument and the terms she used. 'I ask you again: what did you hope to achieve by coming to see me like this?'

Jess settled deeply troubled eyes on him. 'I wanted to be sure you heard the full facts of the case as they happened.'

Regarding her with hard cynical eyes, Cesario loosed a harsh laugh. 'And exactly what were you hoping to gain from this meeting? A full pardon for your father just because I find you attractive? Is that what this encounter is all about?'

Her oval face flamed as though he had slapped her, colour running like a live flame below her skin as he made that statement. It had not even crossed her mind that, with the very many options he had, he might still find her attractive. 'Of course, it's not—'

Cesario's handsome mouth curled with scornful disbelief at that claim. '*Maiala della miseria*…at least tell it like it is! While I may lust after your shapely little body, I don't do it to the extent that I would forgive a crime against me or write off a painting worth more than half a million pounds. You would need to be offering me a great deal more in reparation.'

Jess was gazing back at him in shock, her soft pink lower lip protruding. 'What sort of a man are you? I wasn't offering you sex!' She gasped in horror as she grasped the portent of his words. 'Of course, I wasn't!'

'That's good, because in spite of the scurrilous rumours the British tabloids like to print about me I don't pay for sexual favours or associate with the kind of woman who puts a price on her body,' Cesario declared with an outrageous cool that mocked her seething embarrassment.

'I really *wasn't* offering you sex,' Jess muttered in repeated rebuttal, shattered by that demeaning suggestion.

A well-shaped ebony brow lifted above heavily lashed dark-as-night eyes that remained resolutely unimpressed. 'So, I was just supposed to let your father off the hook for nothing? Does that strike you as a likely deal in such a serious situation?'

'Deal? What *deal*? You're talking like my cousins now. You have a sordid mind,' Jess condemned chokily, her mortification extreme as she snatched up her jacket and began to fight her way into its all-concealing folds. The remainder of her speech emerged in breathless spurts of smarting pride and resentment. 'For your information, I don't sleep around and sex isn't something I would treat like a currency or…or a takeaway meal. *In fact…*'

Unexpectedly amused by her bristling, blushing fury and the discovery that she was much more of a prude than he had had previous cause to suspect, Cesario was striving not to picture her creamy, curvy little body writhing in ecstasy on his silk sheets because he was well aware that that was most probably a fantasy designed to go unfulfilled. 'I'm delighted to hear it.'

'I'm a virgin!' That admission just leapt

off Jess's heated tongue and she froze, appalled that she had let that little-known fact slip. 'Not that that has any relevance when I wasn't offering you sex anyway,' she continued, striving to bury her too intimate confession in a concealing flood of words. 'But I admit that I would have offered you virtually anything else to get my father off the hook. I am *desperate*…'

She lifted her dark head to find Cesario staring back at her with raw incredulity. 'A virgin—you can't be at your age!'

Jess dug hands clenched into fists deep into her pockets and tilted up her chin in defiance of his disbelieving scrutiny. 'I'm not ashamed of it. Why would I be? I didn't meet the right person, it just never happened, and I can live with that.'

But Cesario was not sure he *could* live with the new and tantalising knowledge that she had given him. Suddenly he believed he had finally discovered the source of her discomfort in his radius. Naturally he had assumed she was much more experienced with men and he had treated her accordingly that one evening they had shared. He had probably come on too strong, frightened her off…or very probably his notorious reputation with her sex had done it for him, he reflected in sudden exasperation. Jessica Martin was untouched and, although he had never had a virgin in his bed before, he knew there and then that he would still very much like to be the male who introduced her to that essential missing element in her life. Feeling the taut, charged heaviness of sexual response at his groin in answer to that beckoning tide of erotic imagery, he suppressed a curse and straightened, willing his too enthusiastic body back under firm control again.

'Look, there must be something I can say to you…something I can do to change your mind about Dad's role in this horrible business,' Jess reasoned frantically, literally feeling him disengage from her in the remote set of his shielded eyes and the harsh lines of his lean bronzed features. She was on the edge of panicking. He had asked her what she expected from him and she honestly didn't know. He had not responded with the understanding that she had hoped to ignite with her explanation about her mother's illness and her father's deeply troubled state of mind. He had not responded in the slightest: it had been like crashing into a stone wall at a hundred miles an hour. She had crashed and burned, her persuasive abilities clearly not up to so steep a challenge.

Tears had pooled in her eyes and turned them to liquid silver. Cesario was not a man who responded to tears, but he was unprepared for that feminine softness in her. He had always viewed her as a tough little cookie, assured as she was working in what was so often a man's field, confidently handling his most temperamental stallions while freezing out his every attempt to get closer to her. Yet seeing those tears he still bit back cutting words.

'Promise you'll think over what I've told you,' she urged him in desperation. 'My father is a decent man and he's made a really appalling mistake that you have suffered for. I'm not trying to minimise the loss and distress that you have undergone, but please don't wreck his life over it.'

'I don't let wrongdoers go unpunished. I'm much more in the eye-for-an-eye, tooth-for-a-tooth category,' Cesario delivered, wondering why she was persisting when he had given her so little encouragement. Had she gone on his reputation alone, she would have been expecting him to build a gallows for her father out on the front lawn to stage a public execution.

A hard-hitting businessman, he had never had a name for compassion.

'*Please…*' Jess repeated doggedly, standing by the door as he stopped her advance with one assured hand and reached in front of her to open the door for her with the easy display of effortless courtesy that came so naturally to him. Of course, such smooth civility was totally unfamiliar to her. Her brothers would have broken their necks to get through the door ahead of her and her father had never been taught any such refinements.

'I'm not going to change my mind, but I won't call in the police to tell them what you've told me until tomorrow morning,' Cesario intoned, questioning why he was even willing to cede that breathing space.

From the front hall he watched her drive off in her noisy ancient four-wheel drive. *There must be…something I can do to change your mind…I'm desperate…I would have offered you virtually anything else to get my father off the hook*. And finally he thought about the only thing he really wanted that he couldn't buy and he wondered if he was crazy to even consider her in that light. Was there even enough time left in which he might fulfil that ambition?

He could have her and... *Infierno*, in spite of the other women he had sought out to take the edge off his frustration he *still* wanted Jessica Martin! Given some luck he might also be able to gain what he longed for most from her and on the most fair of terms. In a life that was fast threatening to become shadowed by a bitterness he despised, Cesario was in dire need of a distraction. A woman, the very thought of whom could keep him awake at night with sexual frustration, struck him as the perfect solution.

Of course, it wasn't just desire that motivated him, he reasoned with native shrewdness. She had traits he admired, traits that set her indisputably above most of the women he had known in the past. She was a hard worker who was extremely loyal to her family and she had just willingly sacrificed her pride on their behalf. She devoted all her free time and cash to taking care of animals other people didn't want. Even his wealth, such a magnetic draw to others of her sex, had failed to tempt her into his bed. She was not, by any stretch of the imagination, a gold-digger. Indeed she had good strong standards and he liked that about her. But would those same standards come between her and her family's salvation?

A ruthless calculating smile starting to play around the corners of his hard mouth, Cesario decided to go for the challenge and give her one last chance.

Jess was on duty until nine that evening and she was very tired and low in spirits by the time she drove home with her dogs fast asleep in a huddle in the back of her car. She kept on expecting her mobile phone to ring and for her to hear her distraught mother tell her that her father had been arrested. Cesario di Silvestri had promised to wait until the next day but she didn't believe she could afford to have faith in that proviso because, when she thought about their fruitless exchange, she reluctantly appreciated that she had been guilty of asking him for the impossible.

Even if he didn't personally report her father to the police, Jason and Mark certainly would if they were questioned and implicated in the crime. Her cousins would be eager to spread the blame. The painting had been stolen and there was little hope of retrieving it without the whole sorry tale of its theft being told in detail. There would also be the matter of the insurance claim that would surely be made. Wouldn't the insurers demand assurance that every possible step had been taken to apprehend the perpetrators? So how could Cesario protect her father from being held responsible for his actions?

Letting her other, waiting three dogs out of their fenced run, Jess headed indoors. The cottage was cold and untidy. The old coal-fired kitchen stove had gone out and she sighed, hurrying off to change into clean clothes. She would grab something quick to eat and go out and tend to the animals' needs first. Magic, her deaf Scottish black terrier, bounced round the room as though he were on springs, full of pent-up energy. In between getting changed and washed she repeatedly threw his ball down the hall for him to retrieve. Weed, a skinny grey lurcher, hovered ingratiatingly by the door. Years of loving care had failed to persuade Weed that he could afford to take his happy home for granted. Harley, a diabetic Labrador with a greying muzzle, lay quietly on the floor by the bed, just content to be with her again.

Standing by the kitchen window, Jess ate a sandwich and drank a glass of milk before heading out into the fading light of a late spring evening to take care of the usual evening routine of cleaning, feeding and watering her charges. When she finished and went back indoors, she still had to relight the stove, which always took more than one attempt. Gritting her teeth, she got on with the task.

The phone call came when she was getting ready for bed and so bone-weary that she had all the animation of a zombie.

'It's Cesario…' He reeled off his name in that dark deep rich drawl of his as naturally as if he were in the habit of phoning her, when in actuality it was the very first time he had made a personal call to her.

'Yes?' she queried, cautious in tone as she swallowed back an instinctive urge to ask him angrily who had given him her mobile number.

'Can you come back up to the house at nine tomorrow morning? I have a proposition to put to you.'

'A proposition?' Jess repeated, intense curiosity leaping high inside her to release a tide of speculative thoughts. 'What kind of a proposition?'

'Not the sort that can be discussed over the phone,' he murmured crushingly. 'May I expect you?'

'Yes, tomorrow's my day off.'

Jess came off the phone, her face pale and still, and then she let out an explosive

whoop that startled her pets and jumped up
and down on the spot in a helpless release
of the tension that had held her fast all day.
Evidently, Cesario di Silvestri *had* listened
to her! That phone call had to mean that he
had listened to her and mulled over what she
had told him. Now, in response, he had come
up with a 'proposition', which was really just
another label for that other word 'deal', which
she abhorred.

Acknowledging that truth, her ready sense
of optimism and relief began swiftly to recede
in the face of less comforting thoughts. After
all, an eye-for-an-eye guy would be very unlikely to pardon her imprudent father in return
for nothing. Hadn't he said so himself? What
would be in it for him? Was sex likely to be
involved? With his reputation and the interest
he had previously shown in her, it was difficult to believe it would not be. She winced
in the cosy cocoon of her sensible pyjamas,
thinking of the scars on her abdomen and
back, shivering. It was little wonder that she
had never been keen to strip to reveal those
blemishes to a man or relive the horror of ex-
plaining what had caused them. Sex was out
of the question. In any case, bearing in mind
what she had read in the sleazier newspapers'

'kiss 'n' tell' accounts made by his former lovers, she would never be able to measure up to Cesario's exotic and adventurous habits in the bedroom…

# CHAPTER THREE

CESARIO had a clear view of Jess climbing out of her old Land Rover with several dogs leaping out in her wake.

She had said it was her day off and he had naturally assumed she would dress up for the occasion. Smarten up for their meeting even a little? Surely that was a normal expectation? But she was wearing jeans and a T-shirt roomy enough to fit him below a tweedy woollen cardigan that would not have shamed a scarecrow. Nothing she wore fitted or flattered. He clenched his even white teeth, acknowledging that if, against all the odds, they contrived to reach an agreement, there was definitely going to have to be a lot of compromise on both sides of the fence. She might not do couture, but he definitely *didn't* do dog hairs.

Tommaso beamed at Jess as if they were

old friends and showed her into an imposingly large reception room decked out with almost rock-star glamour in dramatic shades of black and purple. Sumptuous velvet sofas, glass tables and defiantly modern art set the tone. A few minutes later, the older man reappeared with a tray of coffee and biscuits and assured her that his employer would be with her very shortly.

'Business…always business,' he lamented, mimicking a phone to his ear with one hand and rolling his eyes with speaking disapproval.

So jumpy that she couldn't sit still, Jess lifted her cup of coffee and wandered over to examine a colourful painting, struggling to work out if what looked vaguely like a weird face really was meant to be a face. Her taste in art was strictly traditional and very much confined to country landscapes and animal portraits. She would not have given houseroom to Cesario's valuable collection of contemporary art. Her mobile phone trilled and she dug it out one-handed, hastening over to a side table to set down her coffee once she realised that it was her mother, Sharon, calling.

Sharon was in floods of tears, which made it hard to distinguish what she was saying, but

Jess soon picked up the gist. Her father had bared his soul over breakfast and had then beat a very fast masculine retreat from the questions and reproaches hurled at him in the aftermath of his confession. Her mother was in emotional bits, convinced her husband was on the brink of being dragged off to prison for his part in the robbery at the hall.

'That stupid holiday…all this over that stupid holiday I could very well have done without!' Sharon sobbed heartbrokenly. 'And we'll lose the house into the bargain…'

Jess's brows pleated. 'What are you talking about?'

'Well, Mr sodding di Silvestri is not going to let us stay in one of his properties after what your father's done to him, is he?' Sharon wailed. 'I've lived here since I was eighteen and I couldn't bear to lose my home too. And what about your brothers' jobs on the estate? Mark my words, Martin faces won't fit at Halston Hall any more and some way will be found to get rid of us all!'

Jess said what she could to calm her down but Sharon was an emotional woman and a natural pessimist. In Sharon's mind the worst that could happen had happened, and she and her family were already homeless, jobless and broke. Having promised that she would call in later that morning, Jess finally got off the phone and found Cesario watching her from the doorway.

For a split second, she just stared, totally unnerved to find herself the target of that silent scrutiny. Formally clad in a dark business suit and vibrant silk tie, Cesario was effortlessly elegant and intimidating, only the shadow of dark stubble around his strong jaw line making it clear that his morning had commenced at a much earlier hour. She had always thought he was very good-looking but at that moment he looked stunningly handsome, his need for a shave adding a sexy rough edge to his usual immaculate appearance.

'My mother…my father finally worked up the courage to tell her what he had done,' Jess explained awkwardly as she put away her phone, her cheeks pink from her thoughts. 'She's very upset.'

'I'm sure she must be.' Cesario noted the level of stress etched in the tightness of her delicate features. It was an immediate source of satisfaction to him that it was within his power to banish that anxiety from her life. He had lain awake half of the night working out exactly what he wanted and what would work best: a simple straightforward arrangement free of demanding emotions and unrealistic hopes. In the most essential way they would each retain their independence.

'You mentioned a proposition…' she muttered nervously, digging her hands into her pockets, unable to conceal her tension from him

'Hear me out before you give me an answer,' he advised her quietly, registering that, in spite of her unprepossessing clothing, when she looked directly at him she looked so amazingly young and lovely that it was an effort for him to recall what he had planned to say to her. 'And remember that by the time our agreement would come to an end you would be in a most advantageous position.'

She was mystified by that assurance and reference to an agreement, her smooth brow indented, her confusion palpable. But, keen to hear what he had to say, she nodded slowly.

Cesario viewed her with hooded eyes. 'At its most basic, I have come up with a way in which you could help me and in return I would not prosecute your father.'

Eyes wide and hopeful, Jess snatched in an audible breath. 'All right, tell me. How could I help you?'

'I would like to have a child but not in the conventional way,' Cesario explained wryly, his lean aquiline profile taut as she gazed back at him, fine brows rising in surprise. 'I've never been convinced that I can meet one woman and spend the rest of my life with her. On the other hand I believe I could handle a marriage that had a more practical foundation.'

Jess was now frowning more than ever as she struggled to follow what he was telling her and divine how on earth such a topic could relate to her father's predicament. 'How can a marriage be practical?' she asked him uncertainly, convinced that in some way she had misunderstood, because she found it hard to believe that he could possibly be discussing the subject of marriage with her.

'When it's a straightforward contract freed from flowery ideals and expectations like love, romance and permanence,' Cesario outlined with unconcealed enthusiasm. 'If you will agree to have a child with me I will marry you, give you your freedom back within a couple of years and ensure that you need never worry about money again.'

In the grip of astonishment at that sweeping suggestion and his clear conviction that he was making her a generous offer, Jess looked away from him momentarily before turning her head back sharply to stare at him. 'You can't be serious—for goodness' sake, you're young, handsome and rich,' she pointed out. 'There must be any number of women who would be eager to marry you and give you a family.'

'But I don't want a hedonistic gold-digger for a wife or, for that matter, as an unsuitable mother for my child. I want an intelligent, independent woman who will accept my terms and know to expect nothing more lasting from me.'

Not unpleased to be styled both intelligent and independent, Jess stood a little taller. 'But if you're not prepared to commit to a long-term relationship with a woman, why on earth do you want a child?'

'The two are not mutually exclusive. I would commit to my relationship with the child,' Cesario declared with conviction, willing her to see the sound sense behind his arguments. 'I'm not being selfish.'

Jess shook her dark head slowly, her disapproval patent. 'Are you so keen to have a child that you can't wait until you meet the right woman to marry?'

'I would like to say yes and impress you with my credentials as a child-loving male. I do very much want a child of my own,' Cesario proclaimed, his strong sensual mouth compressing with a level of gravity that she had not previously seen in him. 'But that isn't the whole story…'

Unsurprised, Jess nodded acceptance of that admission. 'I thought not.'

'I am the descendant of a long unbroken line of di Silvestris,' Cesario recounted, his brilliant dark eyes narrowing and focusing on a distant point beyond the windows, his attitude one of detachment while his crisp drawl became oddly flat in its delivery. 'My grandfather was immensely proud of that fact. He was obsessed with blood ties and he devoted his life to researching our family tree. Unfortunately he tied his Tuscan estate up in such a way that I cannot legally inherit from my late father unless I have an heir. Male or female, it doesn't matter, but I must have an heir to retain ownership of the family home.'

'My goodness, that was very short-sighted and controlling of him!' Jess commented helplessly. 'I mean, you might have been gay or not remotely interested in having a child.'

'But I'm not gay,' Cesario pointed out drily. 'And I am now choosing to look on this as a project that can be completed.'

'A project…having a baby is a *project*?' Jess repeated in consternation, her thoughts in turmoil.

She thought that it was deeply ironic that he should cherish a desire for something that lay so close to her own heart when they had absolutely nothing else in common. He wanted a child for mainly practical reasons, while she simply wanted a child to love and share her life with. 'I think it would be very wrong for you to bring a child into the world just so that you can inherit some family property.'

'That's one angle, but there are others. I would love my child, who would enjoy a fine education, a supportive family, and who would ultimately inherit everything that I possess,' Cesario responded levelly. 'Any child of mine would enjoy a good life.'

'Why don't you just hire a surrogate mother?' Jess asked bluntly. 'Surely that would make more sense?'

'That wouldn't meet my requirements at all. I come from a conservative background and I prefer that my child be born within what would appear to be a normal marriage for its duration. I also want my son or daughter to have a mother's love and care. I grew up without a mother,' he admitted with an expressive twist of his sensual mouth. 'That's not at all what I want for my own child.'

'I assumed that, in the circumstances you mentioned, you would be seeking full custody of any child that you had,' Jess remarked.

'No. I would not seek more than shared custody and visiting rights. I firmly believe that a child needs a mother to flourish.'

'And a father,' she added abstractedly, thinking of her own childhood when she had adored having her father's attention.

'Of course,' Cesario di Silvestri conceded, but the clipped edge of his voice and the austerity of his expression drew her gaze and she could only wonder what unhappy memory she had contrived to awaken as his lean dark features had shadowed with an expression of regret.

Jess breathed in slow and deep, her brain racing over the outrageous proposition he had outlined, lingering on the pitfalls she saw in the concept and almost immediately rejecting it in full. What he was asking was not only impossible, but insane. She, personally, could not marry a man she did not even like, get into a bed with him and conceive his child. Even thinking about taking part in such a shocking scheme made her tummy somersault and her face burn with the heat of embarrassment.

'You're asking me, but I couldn't possibly marry you,' she declared in a feverish rush.

Cesario dealt her a long measuring look as cool as iced water, for while she might be flustered by the tone of the conversation, he was most definitely not. He also knew that if she rejected his offer he would very much regret having made it. 'You must accept that this is the only option you have and the only offer I have to make you.'

'But it's scarcely a reasonable offer,' Jess complained, her chin coming up in an open challenge.

'I disagree.' His dark eyes gleamed gold below the thick dark screen of his lashes, his lean, strong face implacable. 'In return, I would be making a considerable sacrifice in letting your father and his partners in crime go unpunished. I would also be accepting the permanent loss of my painting without financial compensation as, in this situation, I could not approach the police or make an insurance claim.'

Sobered by that view of the consequences of any agreement being reached, Jess swallowed hard. He had not been joking when he'd talked about offering her a deal. He wanted something in return for the loss of his valuable painting and why not? She thought it unlikely that Cesario di Silvestri was accustomed to being on the losing side of any exchange. And the only thing he seemed to want right now was to become a father without agreeing to the level of commitment or the expectations that would accompany a conventional marriage.

Bearing in mind what she knew about Cesario di Silvestri, that made very good sense to Jess. No woman had ever held his interest for long and it was a challenge to picture him settling down with one woman to start a family in the usual way. On the other hand, choosing a wife and future mother for his child on the basis of cold, hard practicality would sentence him to fewer restrictive ties. A wife who was only pretending to be a proper wife would not require much time or attention either. Yes, as she considered his proposition she could certainly see the advantages from *his* point of view.

And from this practical wife's point of view? A cold contract with a pregnancy and an eventual divorce already organised and agreed upfront? Jess studied her tightly linked hands. Was his proposition really any more distasteful than the conception by artificial means that she had once considered? Much as she longed for a baby, she had not been attracted to the possibility of visiting a sperm bank to be inseminated so that she could conceive a baby by a man she would know next to nothing about. But at least actual intimacy would not have featured in that arrangement.

'If I wasn't so attracted to you I wouldn't even be giving you this option,' Cesario murmured under his breath, the husky timbre of his voice rasping down her taut spinal cord like a physical caress.

Jess glanced up from below her lashes, grey eyes wide and troubled. She felt like someone needing to take cover from a hail of bullets when there was no hiding place available. Her brain was telling her firmly and repeatedly that she could not accept his offer and that some things, not least conception, were sacred and could not be bought. But at the same time when there was no other alternative and her father was in so much trouble...

'If we have not reached an agreement by the time that you leave, I will be calling in the police,' Cesario spelt out with a quietness that was all the more chilling for its lack of volume. 'I now have the proof I need to have charges laid against your father.'

'For goodness' sake, you can't expect any woman to just agree to have a baby with you when there's no existing relationship in place!' Jess exclaimed, shattered by the speed with which he had turned up the pressure on her.

'Why not? Women get married and have children with men they don't love every day of the week. Marriage is a legal contract for good reasons. Many women marry for money, security or status,' Cesario contended. 'You are not being asked to make a huge sacrifice.'

Jess bit down on her impetuous tongue and viewed him from behind furiously resentful silvery eyes for demanding the one thing she could not face agreeing to give him. In her opinion his outrageous offer was just typical of his arrogant, insensitive personality. Giving him a child wasn't a sane doable proposition for a woman like her. She was a very private person and solitary in her outlook. His very lifestyle, habits and tastes were anathema to her and she knew that for a fact before she even tried to add in the horrors of going to bed with a stranger. 'Is that so?'

'Yes, that is so. As far as I'm aware there is no boyfriend in your life to complicate matters and I too am free of any ties. I assure you that if you were to become my wife I would treat you with respect and generosity. This house would be your home. I would not expect you to make a permanent move to Italy on my behalf. In many aspects your life would continue as it always has.'

Jess tried to imagine him in her bed with life continuing as it always had, and almost loosed an overwrought giggle in blunt and incredulous disagreement. But native caution was already beginning to restrain her from a too hasty response.

'Perhaps it is the thought of having to get pregnant that you find most off-putting—'

'No,' she cut in abruptly, surprising herself as much as him. 'I'm at an age when I would very much like a baby, even if it did mean ending up on my own as a single parent. But have you really thought about this idea? You could marry me and I might fail to conceive.'

'That would be fate. I would be disappointed but I would accept it with good grace,' Cesario declared.

The sunshine coming through the window drenched his tall powerful figure in shades of bronze and gold and turned his dark deep-set eyes to gleaming topaz brilliance. As she stared her colour fluctuated and her antipathy to him was only heightened by the quickening of her heartbeat. If she said no, it would be because she did not know how she could possibly hope to fulfil the terms of giving him a positive answer. But she did not feel that she had a choice, or at least she had no choice when faced by the likelihood of her father being imprisoned and the family she adored being torn apart by the fallout from Robert Martin's folly.

Almost thirty years earlier, Robert had promised to bring up Jess as his own child. He had stood faithfully by that promise, even when he'd been censured for not marrying Sharon until her daughter had been almost a year old because everybody had simply assumed that her child was his. In those days, having a child out of wedlock had still been a big deal in a country village and Jess's mother had had a tough time during her months as an unmarried mother. Robert Martin had taken a big gamble when he'd married the woman he loved who, at the time, had willingly admitted that she did not love him. Sometimes, Jess reckoned, in a state of painful anxiety and uncertainty, the only way to move forward was to close your eyes and take a leap in the dark.

'All right…I'll do it!' she breathed with an abruptness that shocked even her as she suppressed her teeming flood of misgivings and tendered agreement without allowing herself to think too hard about what she was doing.

And Cesario di Silvestri actually smiled, but not with the usual curl of his handsome mouth that had on previous occasions left her unimpressed. He gave her a dazzling smile powered by enough charisma to float a battleship, his lean, darkly handsome features energised by that expression on his wide, sensual mouth.

'You won't regret this,' he asserted with confidence, reaching for her hand to mark their accord. Just before he released her fingers he noticed the line of paler scar tissue along the back of her hand and asked abruptly, 'What happened here?'

Jess froze and paled, her heart suddenly beating frantically fast. 'Oh, an accident…a long time ago,' she heard herself say, only just resisting the temptation to yank her hand free again.

'It was a nasty one,' Cesario remarked, releasing her fingers.

He had picked an unfortunate moment in which to notice that scar and rouse bad memories. Indeed Jess had barely agreed to marry him before she fell into the turmoil of doubt and regret, but she rammed back those feelings and simply nodded, focusing her thoughts on the future rather than on that distressing episode from her past. The end would justify the means, she told herself urgently. Cesario would get what he wanted but so would *she*. Her child would still be her child to keep and he or she would benefit from a father. She would not think about the bedroom end of things, she absolutely would not think about that aspect until she was forced to do so.

'I'll get my staff to make a start on the wedding arrangements,' Cesario informed her.

Jess studied him in dismay. 'You *are* in a hurry.'

'Naturally…I wouldn't want you to change your mind, *piccola mia*,' Cesario sent her a winging appraisal, his beautiful mouth taking on that sardonic curl she had always disliked. 'And we have no reason to waste time before we embark on our project, have we?'

'I suppose not,' she mumbled as she bent to lift her jacket.

Cesario extended his hand and, when she failed to grasp his intention, simply and coolly removed the jacket from her grasp before shaking it open for her to put on. Colouring as she finally realised what he was doing, she turned to slide her arms into the sleeves, tensing beneath the familiarity when he tugged her hair out from below the collar where it was caught.

'I'll look forward to seeing your hair loose,' he told her with husky anticipation.

And something in his dark voice and the intensity of his appraisal as she turned her head spooked her so that she backed off a hasty step. No man had ever had the power to make her so conscious of her own body, and around him she always felt clumsy and naïve.

Cesario ignored the arms she had crossed in front of her like a defensive barrier and touched her cheek with a reproving brown forefinger. 'You're going to be my wife. You will have to get used to being touched by me.'

'And how am I supposed to do that?' Jess questioned, infuriated by the fact that at such speed and with even less effort he had reduced her to a state of almost adolescent awkwardness in his presence.

Ignoring the distrustful vibrations that she was putting out, Cesario closed his hand over one of hers and tugged her inexorably closer. 'Try relaxing first…'

Her teeth momentarily chattered together behind her closed lips as if she had been plunged suddenly into an icy bath.

'I'm only going to kiss you,' he imparted silkily.

Jess froze, her silvery eyes flickering with dismay at even that prospect. 'No—'

'We have to start somewhere, *piccola mia*.'

But he surprised her by releasing her hand and she snatched it back and was about to retreat further until it occurred to her that she could no longer afford to follow her own inclinations where he was concerned. If she couldn't even allow him to kiss her, he would naturally assume that she couldn't handle their agreement and he would withdraw his proposal. She froze like a bird confronted by a hungry stalking cat.

Cesario laughed softly in triumph and colour ran like a fire up over her cheekbones. She gazed up at him, properly aware for almost the first time of how much taller and heavier he was, six feet plus inches of lean, power-packed muscle. Her colour drained away, silvery eyes veiling as she reminded herself that she had no reason to fear him, but her body wasn't listening to her brain, for it was angling backwards without her volition, almost tipping her off balance. Her heart was positively thundering in her ears.

'There are some things I'm very good at,' Cesario delivered with innate assurance. 'And this is one of them, *piccola mia*.'

And his mouth slid across her sealed-shut lips as lightly as a dandelion seed borne by the breeze. She had expected passion, but he defied her expectations and her heart set up an even louder thump behind her breastbone, the pace speeding up as he brushed his knowing mouth back over hers and the extent of her tension made her rigid. The tip of his tongue scored that seam of denial and her body came

alive when she was least prepared for it, a
jerky quiver of feminine response slivering
through her with almost painful effect as she
parted her lips to let him kiss her properly.
It was slow and hot and very thorough and
it shook her up because her nipples pinched
into hard little buds and her breasts swelled
so that her bra felt as if it was constricting her
ability to breathe. As his tongue delved with
erotic skill into the sensitive interior of her
mouth, moist heat surged between her thighs
and she trembled.

'That's enough,' she said shakily, her hands
rising against his broad shoulders to push him
back from her. Feverishly flushed, she found
it hard to accept that once again she had enjoyed the feel of his mouth on hers. She had
thought it was a fluke the last time he had
kissed her and she had been intimidated by
the pent-up passion she could feel in him.

'No, it's only the beginning,' Cesario
husked, smouldering golden eyes fringed
by dense black lashes roving boldly over her
averted face so that when she glanced up, she
flinched at that visual connection and hurriedly looked away.

'This wedding you mentioned,' Jess remarked hurriedly, keen to move on to a less

controversial subject because she was taken aback by the way he was looking at her. She stifled an urge to shiver because she felt cornered. She was not so naïve that she didn't recognise the force of his desire for her and she could hardly afford to knock the source of her apparent appeal when it was probably the main reason he was offering her a wedding ring and her father's freedom. 'When would it take place?'

'As soon as it can be arranged—it *will* be a proper wedding,' Cesario decreed without hesitation. 'With the dress, the big guest list, the whole bridal show.'

'Is that really necessary?' Jess pressed uneasily, wincing at the prospect of having to play the blushing bride for an audience of posh strangers.

'It won't look like a normal marriage otherwise,' he pointed out.

'Oh, my goodness, what am I going to tell my family?' she suddenly gasped in an appalled undertone.

'Not the truth, for that is only for you and I to know,' Cesario spelt out in a tone of warning.

He had just given her an impossible embargo, but Jess was already reaching the

conclusion that it was better not to blurt out
unwary comments around Cesario. She knew
even then that she would tell her mother the
truth, but that she would present it in an edited
version to satisfy her father's curiosity without
making the older man feel responsible for her
predicament. She breathed in deep and slow,
reminding herself firmly of the positive aspects to her situation and repeating them over
and over to herself in a soothing mantra. Her
father would not pay the price for his stupidity
and her family circle would stay intact. She
would hopefully end up with the baby she had
long dreamt of having and she would even
have that all important wedding ring on her
finger first, since her mother set great store
on a woman being married in advance of the
arrival of children.

So what if it was a project rather than a
wedding? She could cope with that. She
was very realistic and, if he was as good at
everything else as he was at kissing, given
time she would surely come to terms with the
more intimate aspects of their relationship.
Women didn't always marry just for love,
she reminded herself doggedly, and neither
did men, as Cesario was about to prove. If
such a marriage was good enough for him

when she was convinced that he could have so many more exciting options, it should be good enough for her as well.

'Why did you choose me for this?' she heard herself ask without warning.

His dense lashes swooped low over his brilliant dark gaze. 'Ask me on our wedding night,' he advised, a piece of advice that not unnaturally silenced her…

# CHAPTER FOUR

'I LIKE the dress with the full skirt best,' Jess repeated doggedly, ignoring the raised brows of Melanie, the hip fashion stylist Cesario had hired to work with her in what bore all the hallmarks of a tip-to-toe makeover.

Jess, however, was determined to at least choose her own wedding gown. 'It suits me,' she added.

'It's very, very pretty,' Sharon Martin agreed with unconcealed delight at her daughter's choice.

'Well, if you like bling,' Melanie said drily, encouraging the saleswoman to display the dress so that the pearl-beaded bodice and the scattered crystals on the skirt sparkled in the light, her lack of enthusiasm palpable. 'It has certainly got buckets of bling.'

Jess had surprised herself with her choice. Although her taste generally ran to the plain, she had fallen head over heels in love with the unashamedly romantic wedding gown. Melanie's efforts to persuade her client to pick a restrained satin column style instead had fallen on stony ground.

On that score, though, it had to be admitted that Jess had enjoyed a rare victory. She had already had to accept an entire trousseau of new garments for her up-and-coming role as the wife of an international tycoon and her preferences had often been politely ignored. Cesario was a perfectionist who dotted every i and crossed every t, while Jess was someone who never ever sweated the small stuff if she could help it. And arguing on the phone about something as unimportant as clothes with a male as single-minded and accustomed to getting his own way as Cesario was, she had learned, exhausting and ultimately pointless.

It was a fact that Jess had taken virtually no interest in clothes and cosmetics since that traumatic episode in her late teens when she had decided that it was safer and much more comfortable not to dress to attract male attention. Now willing to admit that she was out of date with regard to fashion and the art of self-presentation, she had agreed to accept

advice and grooming. As a result, her un-
controllable black waterfall of curls had been
shaped and tamed and her brows plucked.
While she could see that her appearance had
improved and her hair was much more man-
ageable, she was appalled that the time she
had already had to spend in the beauty salon
was now being extended into the territories of
waxing, facials, manicure and pedicure sessions. Was there no end to the vanity sessions
she was expected to endure? Her colleagues
at the veterinary practice had pulled her leg
unmercifully as the ugly duckling—as she
saw herself as—was ruthlessly repackaged
into a would-be swan.

Although only three weeks had passed
since Jess had agreed to marry Cesario di
Silvestri, the comfortable groove of her life
was fast being erased. The wedding was set
for a date only ten days away and Cesario
had been abroad on business almost from
the day they had agreed to marry. A giant
diamond cluster, delivered by special cou-
rier, now adorned her ring finger and an announcement about their engagement had appeared in an upscale broadsheet newspaper
that nobody Jess knew read. In response to
that first public reference to her new position,

a photographer had just the day before popped up from behind a hedge to take a ghastly picture of her returning to the surgery after a difficult calving, bedraggled and dirty with her hair like a bird's nest. The subsequent picture, comically entitled *Jet-Set Bride?*, had appeared that very morning in a down-market tabloid. Jess had merely pulled a face when a colleague showed it to her, because getting messed up in her field of work was an occupational hazard. Cesario, however, had requested that she meet him for lunch to discuss the matter.

'Don't go falling in love with Cesario,' Sharon advised her daughter as she was being driven home, shooting Jess a troubled glance. 'It worries me that you will and then you'll get hurt...'

'As it won't be a real marriage I'm not going to fall for him,' Jess fielded with a sound of dismissive amusement, wondering if she had made a mistake in telling her mother the truth about Cesario's proposal of marriage.

'Don't you fool yourself. If you have a baby with the man, it'll be just as real as any other marriage,' her mother forecast ruefully. 'And I know you. You have a softer heart than you like to show.'

'I'm also almost thirty-one years old and I've never been in love in my life,' her daughter reminded her crisply.

'Only because you let that creep at university put you off men!' Sharon Martin retorted with an expressive grimace that recognised her daughter's sudden pallor and tension. 'Cesario is a very handsome guy and I think it would be easier for you than you think to lose your head over him. You'll be living together, sharing your lives, for goodness' sake!'

'But we won't be sharing anything but a desire to have a child,' Jess pronounced flatly, her cheekbones colouring as she made that point. She had told her mother everything and sworn her to silence for her father's sake. Robert Martin had swallowed the contrived story that Jess had been seeing Cesario on the quiet without telling anyone and he saw no reason why even a billionaire should not be bowled over by his beautiful daughter. 'Cesario made that quite clear, Mum. He likes his own space. He wants a child but that's the extent of it. He certainly doesn't want a wife who might get too comfortable in the role.'

'I know…it's a marriage of convenience, just like your dad and I made…'

'Not at all like you and Dad,' Jess protested

firmly. 'Dad was in love with you, even if you didn't feel the same way at the time. That made a big difference. Cesario and I have already agreed to a divorce before we even get married.'

'It's not as easy to keep emotions out of things as you think it will be,' Sharon retorted, unconvinced by her daughter's arguments.

Jess watched her mother walk into her terraced house in the centre of the village before reversing her old Land Rover to drive over to Halston Hall and meet Cesario for lunch. Once Sharon Martin had adjusted to the shock of her daughter's confidences, which Jess had presented in a very positive way, she had gotten excited by the prospect of the wedding and the very fact that her beloved daughter was about to marry a very wealthy and influential man.

Jess drove past the public entrance to the extensive parkland that Cesario had thrown open to the public. It contained a lake, a playground he had had built at great expense, wooded walks and picnic spots. His tenants, employees and neighbours were free to stage events with permission in the grounds as well. It was ironic that a foreigner like Cesario di Silvestri had already done more for the community than the Dunn-Montgomery family had done in several centuries of having owned the great house. The man she was about to marry for the most practical of reasons had an admirably public-spirited side to his nature, she acknowledged reluctantly.

Aware that her heart was thumping so fast it left her breathless, Jess climbed out of her car and headed for the arched front doors of the hall. She was already running through a mental checklist. The engagement ring was in place, her hair tidy and she was dressed in an elegant pair of trousers teamed with a lace-edged grey cashmere twinset. All she lacked was a set of ladylike pearls and the thought made her grin. That morning she had barely recognised her reflection in the mirror. Being married to Cesario was going to be like taking on a new and taxing job with different rules from those she was accustomed to following.

Tommaso greeted her with his usual enthusiasm and swept her through to a reception room a little less opulent than the drawing room.

'Jessica…' Cesario strolled towards her with the pure predatory grace that always contrived to draw her attention to the lean, well-balanced flow of his powerful body.

The instant her gaze found his lean, darkly handsome features she remembered the heat and taste of that wide sensual mouth on hers and hot pink warmed her cheekbones. He was too good-looking, way too good-looking, she thought in vexation, meeting dark deep-set golden eyes fringed by ebony lashes longer than her own. She felt as if a stream of liquid fire were slowly travelling from the tautening tips of her breasts down into her pelvis to create a pool of wicked waiting warmth there. It was an unnerving sensation and it overpowered her earlier sense of being in control.

Cesario ran his intent scrutiny over her petite figure, now enhanced by garments that actually fitted her delicate proportions; he was entranced by the beauty of her fine-boned face and the lush heaviness of the ebony curls now falling round her cheekbones. 'You look amazing…'

'I think that's a major exaggeration,' Jess told him awkwardly, hugely uncomfortable with the compliment.

'Not when you compare it to this,' Cesario remarked drily, lifting the newspaper lying on the coffee table to display the photo of her in muddy bespattered clothing and wellington boots. 'How can you let yourself be seen out and about looking like that?'

That question hit Jess like a slap in the face and she bridled, tipping her head back to stare at him. 'I had just spent three hours at a calving. The calf was dead but the mother just survived. I was filthy and exhausted—that's what my working day is like sometimes.'

'In your role as my future wife I will expect you to consider your image,' Cesario drawled as smoothly as though she had not spoken up in her own defence.

Jess's chin took on a defiant angle. 'I can't help it if a photographer lies in wait to catch me looking my worst. I couldn't care less about that sort of silly stuff.'

'We do not need to discuss this. The bottom line is that I will not accept you appearing in public looking like a tramp,' Cesario informed her in a tone of cold finality.

'Then we've got a big problem,' Jess countered, refusing to yield an inch of ground in the face of his unjust censure. 'My job is often dirty and I often have to work outdoors. I have no intention of giving my job up just so that I can always look like a perfect doll for your benefit.'

'I'm not asking you to look like a doll,' Cesario fielded in exasperation, marvelling that she could be so indifferent to appearing in print in such a state.

'Then how is it that after only three weeks of being engaged to you, I already feel like a dress-up doll? You seem to think I have nothing better to do with my time than shop or sit in a beauty salon enduring endless time-wasting treatments,' Jess condemned thinly, her grey eyes darkening with anger to the colour of steel, because she felt he was being most unfair when she had already obediently jumped through so many hoops to smarten up.

'Until I intervened you made no effort with your appearance at all. A woman with healthy self-esteem wants to look her best,' Cesario contended grimly. 'What's wrong with yours?'

'The level of my self-esteem is none of your business!' Jess fielded flatly, her temper rising, as she was annoyed that he had noticed that she did not like her looks to attract attention. 'I'm just an ordinary working woman.'

'You work so many hours that you haven't got time to be a woman,' Cesario delivered, dark eyes gleaming gold with displeasure because she was refusing to accept his point of view. 'I had no idea how long a day you worked until I began phoning you. You're hardly ever at home and when you are you're chasing after those animals you keep. It's ridiculous.'

A flush of indignant disbelief slowly washing up over her face at that summary criticism, Jess shot him a furious look of resentment. 'You said you wanted an intelligent, independent woman but obviously you lied. My career is the most important thing in my life.'

'I thought your family was.'

The reminder sobered her but it also felt as though he were cracking a whip over her head to remind her of the terms of their agreement. Aggravated, she compressed her soft full lips. 'If you try to interfere with my job, this arrangement isn't going to work for either of us,' she warned him tautly. 'For goodness' sake, you said you'd want a divorce in a couple of years, so why should you try to hinder my career?'

'I also want a wife I see occasionally and you are rarely available in the evening or at weekends.'

'Do you know what the *real* problem here

is? You want a little wifey-slave who focuses only on her appearance and on you, a domestic goddess with nothing better to do with her time.'

'A boudoir goddess would be more my style, *piccola mia*,' Cesario derided with a sardonic smile. 'You're not being practical. At the very least, you'll have to reduce your hours of employment to a more acceptable level.'

'That's out of the question!'

'Perhaps while you remain a comparatively junior employee, but if you were to buy into the veterinary practice as a partner, you would have more control over the hours you work.'

At that unexpected suggestion, Jess rested stunned eyes on him. 'What on earth are you talking about?'

'I will buy you a partnership.'

'No…*no*, you will not!' Jess decreed in a shaking voice, so angry she barely trusted herself to speak. 'Stay away from the surgery and don't you dare meddle. My goodness, you're unbelievable! If you can't immediately have what you want you try to buy it!'

'When I see a problem I come up with a solution,' Cesario contradicted in a tone of ice-cased steel. 'And, right now, it is obvious that you have three options.'

'Three...*options*?' Jess parroted with wrathful emphasis.

'You allow me to purchase you a partnership, or you ask to work part-time hours *or* you quit altogether,' Cesario enumerated, watching her flinch in disbelief with an impassive countenance. 'Something has to give in your current schedule. At present there isn't room in it for a marriage, a husband and the conception of a child.'

'I agreed to marry you, not let you take over my entire life!' Jess snapped back at him in raw rampant incredulity. 'Or tell me what to do and what not to do!'

'*Madre di Dio*...take a deep breath, calm down and think about what I'm saying,' Cesario urged, stunned by the force of her fury. 'You will have to make changes.'

'No, I'm not about to listen to another bloody word of this nonsense!' Jess lashed back at him, more angry than she had ever been in her life and unable to tolerate his evident conviction that he now had the right to mess about with her career. Swivelling on her heel, she headed back to the door, prompted by some sixth-sense caution that warned her to get out before she lost her temper entirely.

'If you walk out in a tantrum, you needn't bother coming back,' Cesario pronounced with a chilling hauteur that hurt and stung as much as an ice burn. 'My cousin, Stefano, and his wife are waiting in the next room to meet you at lunch.'

Jess froze and gritted her teeth like a feral cat ready to hiss and snarl in attack. He had a knack no other man had ever equalled— he filled her to overflowing with pure rage. She knotted her hands into fists by her side, shocked by the tempest of fury gripping her and barely able to credit that she had been the most laid-back of personalities.

'I like to deal with potential pitfalls in advance,' Cesario asserted in soft and low continuance.

Just at that moment Jess imagined pushing him off the edge of a cliff and had the funniest suspicion that if he went over he would take her with him. She wondered in genuine horror how on earth she would ever live with him. Her narrow spine still turned to him, she breathed in slow and deep, praying for calm and composure while she reminded herself doggedly of all she stood to lose. And,

embarrassingly, it was not her father's plight
that came first to mind, it was the baby she
had been trying to picture at dawn that morning. A little boy, a little girl; she didn't care as
long as her baby was healthy. Her breathing
began slowing in speed.

'Obviously I've taken you by surprise with
this.'

Grey eyes still openly alight with hostility,
Jess spun back to him. 'I live alone, I do as
I like. I'm not used to anyone trying to limit
me.'

A drumbeat of tension and reluctant arousal
assailing him like an erotic pulse, Cesario
studied her vivid and mutinous little face and
marvelled that even those spiky defences of
hers and the mud had contrived to keep her
single and unattached for so long. For a few
moments there, he had genuinely thought
she would stalk out like a tigress breaking
free of her cage. Her temperament was much
more emotional and passionate than he had
appreciated. It was a discovery that should
have worried him but in reality it turned him
on. Cesario was already beginning to learn
the hard lesson that what he needed was not
always what he wanted.

'But you will consider those options and

make a decision,' he breathed huskily, unable to resist the suspicion that having got her metaphorically back into the cage again he was now deliberately provoking her.

The dark melting timbre of his accented drawl shimmied over Jess like a sudden disarming caress, awakening the awareness that she was accustomed to suppressing whenever he was in her radius. In severe discomfiture she shifted off one foot onto the other, but she still recognised the fullness of her breasts and the pinch as her nipples tightened followed by the dragging ache of longing between her legs. It was lust, just good old-fashioned lust, a natural and normal human prompting and not worth getting upset about, she told herself urgently. But that reassuring thought did not have quite the soothing effect she hoped it would because Cesario di Silvestri was the *only* man who had ever affected her that way. One look the first time she met him and she had burned, and the knowledge still infuriated her and intimidated her in his presence.

In a desperate effort to throw off the effect he was having on her Jess struggled to continue the conversation without giving ground. 'I'll think over what you've said.'

'And make a decision...'

'And you really want that decision right now, don't you?' Jess blasted back at him before she could stamp down her temper again. 'You're so ridiculously impatient!'

Cesario looked levelly back at her, his eyes very dark and uninformative below the shade of his lush lashes. 'We have a great deal to accomplish in a short space of time. I need your co-operation to do this.'

Mortified by her imperfect grip on her anger when he was as much in control as he had ever been, Jess nodded stiffly.

'You will obviously move your animal rescue operation to Halston as well.'

As Jess parted her lips in shock at that supposition, which she had not even considered, Cesario dealt her a silencing appraisal. 'Nothing else would make sense. I assumed you would wish to retain that interest and I have already spoken to my estate manager.'

'Have you indeed?' Jess cut in before she could swallow back the hot, hasty words.

'Naturally. You could scarcely continue your work at a property several miles away and why should you want so inconvenient an arrangement? Land here will be put at your disposal and you may of course order custom-made buildings to house your charges.

Naturally I will cover all the costs. I would also suggest the hire of at least one full-time employee.'

A choky little sound of incredulity escaped Jess and she viewed him with enraged silvery eyes. 'Anything else?'

'We will be staying in Italy for around six weeks after the wedding. You will need a trustworthy staff member to take care of your animals.'

Jess folded her arms with a defensive jerk because it was preferable to throwing something or walking out in what he had earlier clearly seen as a childish tantrum. He thought of everything. No corner of her life was to be safe from his interference and he was laying that on the line. He was in the driver's seat now, not her.

Cesario searched her taut face. The vibrations in the atmosphere were explosive. He wanted to skim his fingers through that wonderful hair, run a soothing hand across those rigid little shoulders and tell her that if she pleased him the sky was the limit, because there was virtually nothing he would not do for her, nothing he would not give. But that was not possible in the circumstances and might well have given her dangerous ideas.

His inherent caution kept those spontaneous urges under control.

'Come and meet Stefano and his wife, Alice. They're my oldest friends,' Cesario murmured, a light hand at her spine guiding her across the hall towards the drawing room.

For an instant he paused and she looked questioningly up at his lean dark face, sexual awareness rolling in around her in an almost suffocating flood of impressions. The scent of his expensive cologne drifted into her nostrils. She loved the smell of it, had only to catch a whiff of that citrus-based aroma to think of him. His strong jaw line was slightly rough with dark stubble and her fingers tingled with the need to touch him. Her body hummed in readiness as though he had thrown a switch. Every time he got close her reaction was stronger and more unnerving. She wanted him to kiss her; she wanted him to kiss her so badly that not being kissed *hurt*.

'I know, *piccola mia*,' Cesario purred soft and low, brilliant eyes bronze with sensual appreciation, a slight catch in his low-pitched voice. 'But we have company for lunch.'

Jess wasn't quite sure she had actually *heard* that assurance, for it implied that he had known exactly how she was feeling and the suspicion appalled her. Her face was flushed when she entered the drawing room to find a stockily built, balding man in his thirties with lively brown eyes advancing on her. His wife was a tall, slender blonde, so eye-catchingly lovely that Jess found that she was staring.

'I've been really looking forward to meeting you,' Alice di Silvestri confided with a warm friendly smile, these first words revealing that she was American.

And Cesario curved an entire arm round Jess, who stiffened before appreciating that her role of happy bride-to-be had acquired its first audience and found that she was smiling back. She cast off the weight of anger, anxiety and stress that had until that instant been weighing her down and crushing her spirits. She had come through and survived far worse than a convenient marriage, she reminded herself with stubborn resolution. Nothing that Cesario could throw at her was likely to trip her up…

# CHAPTER FIVE

'YOU look as pretty as a picture,' Robert Martin pronounced, a betraying brightness to his eyes as he admired Jess in her wedding gown from the lounge doorway.

Restive in her unusually feminine finery, Jess peered at her reflection in the hall mirror, noting that the make-up artist had done a heck of a job in giving her a youthful, dewy look, while the hairstylist had worked a miracle transforming her teeming curls into soft shiny ringlets that fell round her bare shoulders. A splendid diamond tiara worthy of a princess glittered against the dark backdrop of her hair, courtesy of Cesario, who had sent it with the information that it was a family heirloom. She smiled wryly at the memory, wondering if he had been afraid she might think it was a personal gift, because she cherished no such illusions about her bridegroom.

Cesario di Silvestri had no plans to bring anything personal into their relationship. Her bridegroom was ruthless, ferociously self-disciplined and clever. When it came to his track record with women, he might have a very well-documented and volatile libido but in spirit Jess believed he was essentially cold. He might want a child. But that child, she was convinced, would have to look to her for the warmth of human kindness and affection. Cesario planned his every move, foreseeing every difficulty and then judging how best to deal with it. He was a control freak, a demanding personality with very high standards and expectations. Nothing less than the best would satisfy him in any field, which begged the question, why was a man who could have married any number of rich, beautiful, society women settling for a country veterinary surgeon from a much more ordinary background?

Was her winning factor her sex appeal? Her cheeks warmed. Or was it because she had once said no and refused to see him again? Could any guy be that petty? She could not see herself as a femme fatale, but what else but her looks could have sustained his ongoing interest? Was it offensive to be that desirable to a man? She found it hard to think of sexual desirability as an accolade. After all, being a man's object of desire had once long ago almost cost Jess her life and she shivered, suddenly chilled by traumatic memories that she very rarely allowed herself to recall.

Her niece and nephew, Emma and Harry, four and five years old respectively, looked adorable and were the perfect antidote to her briefly dark thoughts. Emma wore a floral-print bridesmaid's dress, while Harry was smartly dressed as a pageboy. Their mother, Leondra, who had married Jess's youngest brother when she fell pregnant at eighteen, had agreed to act as a matron of honour, although she had complained bitterly over the lack of a hen night to mark the end of Jess's life as a single woman. Jess had not had the nerve to tell her sister-in-law that she was expecting to be single again sooner than anyone other than her clued-up mother might expect.

'If only *he* could see you now,' her father proclaimed in a fond undertone while Leondra was talking to her children. 'He would im-mediately regret never having known you.'

'I don't think so.' Unhappily reminded of a rejection that had cut her in two when she was only nineteen years old, Jess stiffened defensively. The identity crisis she had undergone during that troubled period in her life had taught her not to build fantasy castles in the air. *Better the devil you know than the devil you don't,* she chanted inwardly, because she had learned to be grateful for the years of love and care she had received from the father she had once taken for granted. She would have hugged the older man had she not been afraid of spoiling her make-up. Just for once, she wanted to look perfect. There was nothing wrong with her self-esteem, she reflected impatiently, she was simply determined to grace her beautiful gown at the altar. For her own benefit, *not* for Cesario's.

After all, some day she would be showing the photos that would be taken of the occasion to her child. She had to believe in that, had to keep her thoughts firmly fixed on that ultimate all-important goal of having a baby. At the end of the day, a child would be what really mattered. Only it would not quite cover the wedding night and how she felt about sharing that kind of intimacy with a man who didn't love her.

Her tummy flipped when she thought about Cesario seeing her scars for the first time.

In her opinion they weren't *that* bad. There was the chance that given enough darkness he mightn't even notice them. On the other hand, this was a guy accustomed to some of the world's most beautiful women and in every other way he was very much a perfectionist. And she was, by no stretch of the imagination, perfect any more. Stifling the kernel of panic deep down inside her, she struggled to overcome the sudden fear that he might be repelled by her flawed body. Some people were repelled by scarring and they probably couldn't even help reacting that way. As the car arrived to take her to the church she suppressed the rolling tide of insecure thoughts threatening to engulf her. Instead she scolded herself and acknowledged the futility of looking for trouble in advance.

Her heart was beating like thunder when she looked at the packed pews of the little flower-bedecked church of Charlbury St Helens, which lay only a hundred yards away from her parents' home. Lack of space in the nave had meant restricting the number of guests able to see the ceremony. When she caught a glimpse of Cesario standing so tall, dark and straight at the altar, she found it hard to get oxygen into her lungs. And then suddenly and without any warning at all, and in a spirit of sharp regret, she found that she was wishing that her wedding were for real, an occasion where two people in love shared their vows for a shared and productive future. The unemotional exchange of needs that she had agreed with Cesario was on another plane entirely and just then she felt incredibly lonely. A surge of over-emotional tears stung the backs of her eyes.

'Your bride looks gorgeous,' Stefano remarked admiringly at his cousin's elbow.

And Cesario stopped playing it cool and turned to get his own view. He felt the word didn't stretch anywhere far enough to do justice to the vision of Jessica in the full-skirted sparkling gown with a corset bodice that moulded her slim curves and defined her tiny waist. So stunning was she with her light grey eyes shining, her soft mouth unusually tremulous and full and her heavy mass of hair falling below the tiara that he barely registered the aggravation of her arriving at the altar on the arm of the man who had let thieves into his house.

Jess met Cesario's brilliant dark eyes and experienced a sizzling sensation in her pelvis that was unnervingly similar to an electric shock. Breathing rapidly, she averted her attention from him and concentrated studiously on the middle-aged priest's opening preamble. The ceremony was short and familiar, similar to a number of friends' weddings she'd attended in recent years, but she still could not quite accept that *this* time she was the bride. Her hand shook a little when Cesario first grasped it and she stopped breathing altogether when he slid the slim band of gold onto her wedding finger. His handsome mouth brushed her cheek in a light salutation and then they walked down the aisle, guests beaming at them as though they had done something terribly clever. She remembered to smile for the benefit of the congregation, which, aside of her mother, had no idea that she was not a normal, happy bride.

'You look amazing in that dress, *mia bella*,' Cesario commented during the drive back to Halston Hall where the reception was being held.

'And I picked it all by myself.' Jess could not resist letting him know. 'The stylist wanted me to wear something plainer and more formal.'

'You made the right choice.'

Relaxing a little, Jess sighed. 'With all this

fuss going on around us, it's hard to remember that it's all fake.'

Cesario frowned. 'It is *not* fake,' he contradicted.

*Fake, fake, fake!* she wanted to shout at him in defiant disagreement, but, suspecting such a response would annoy him, she managed to resist the impulse.

'We are now husband and wife and we will live as such.' Cesario delivered his different opinion in a tone of powerful conviction.

But Jess was stubborn and hard to impress and she wrinkled her nose. 'A temporary marriage could never feel real,' she said quietly, thinking of the very long, wordy legal contract she'd had to sign a couple of weeks earlier before the marriage could go ahead.

This prenuptial contract had made it very clear that the marriage was more of a commercial arrangement than anything else. The terms of the eventual divorce had been laid out with equal clarity with regard to income, property and the custody and care of any child born to them. No woman who'd had to sign such a detailed document could have cherished any romantic illusions about the nature of the marriage she was about to enter.

Cesario set his white even teeth together.

'Talk of that variety is premature. We don't know as yet when our marriage will end. That's not the aspect you should be concentrating on right now.'

But Jess was no more eager to think about the mechanics of getting pregnant. What if it simply didn't happen? What a nightmare that would be! For a start, it was the only reason he was marrying her and, from her own point of view, it was the only feature that made the whole agreement supportable. She wouldn't think about her wedding night, instead she would think about the baby she was desperate to hold in her arms. Only she discovered as she stood in line to greet their guests in the Great Hall of the Elizabethan house that she could not wipe Cesario's starring role in that future development from her mind and her nervous tension began to mount again.

The exhausting day continued and, having had little practice as a social butterfly, Jess found it a strain to laugh and talk and smile continuously with strangers, many of whom were undoubtedly curious to see what was so special about her that she had managed to get a male of Cesario's reputation to the altar. If only they'd had access to the truth, she thought wryly, standing behind a door in a quiet corner when she finally managed to escape the crush for a few minutes. At least the meal, the speeches and the first dance were over, she reflected ruefully, grateful that the spotlight of attention was no longer on the bride and groom quite so much. She gulped down a glass of champagne in the hope that the alcohol would help her to feel a little more relaxed and light-hearted, for Cesario had already suggested twice that she 'loosen up'. Her natural shyness and reserve seemed to be a disadvantage around him.

'I can't believe that Alice is being *so* two-faced,' Jess heard a female voice state with perceptible scorn. 'I don't believe for a moment that she is really pleased that Cesario has finally found a wife.'

'Oh, neither do I,' agreed another. 'After all, Alice was once utterly crazy about Cesario and she only married Stefano because *he* adores *her.*'

'I can understand why she did it, though. She'd been with Cesario for two years, there was no sign of him making a commitment and she wasn't getting any younger. Don't forget she's a few years older than he is and she didn't waste any time in having children with Stefano.'

'I heard that Cesario was devastated when she walked out on him for his cousin.'

The other woman laughed in disbelief. 'Can you imagine Cesario being devastated over a woman? If he'd cared about Alice that much he'd have married her when he had the chance.'

'Most men would consider a woman like Alice a keeper.'

'As you can see by his choice of bride, though, Cesario is *not* most men,' her companion said scornfully. 'Granted she's got the looks, but nobody had ever heard of her before the invitations arrived.'

'Why would we have heard of her? She looks after his horses!'

Jess moved away from the doorway in haste before she could be seen. Looks after his horses indeed, she thought in exasperation, recalling her long years of study and training for her career in veterinary medicine. She had no reason, though, to disbelieve what she had innocently overheard and she was taken aback to learn that Alice and Cesario had once been lovers. An affair that Cesario allowed to last for two years must have been serious, although the beautiful blonde had somehow ended up married to his cousin instead. Even more surprisingly, that development did not appear to have damaged the friendship between the two men.

'Have a drink,' her mother urged, pressing a champagne glass into her daughter's nerveless hand. 'You hardly ate anything of the wedding breakfast and you are as white as a ghost.'

'I'm fine,' Jess asserted automatically, her eyes anxiously scanning the knots of people in search of Cesario's tall dark head.

Ironically he was on the dance floor with Alice, the two of them so busy talking that they were circling very slowly. Stefano was watching his wife and his cousin from the top table, a troubled expression etching lines to his face

'What's wrong?' Sharon Martin prompted, reading her daughter's tension easily.

Jess continued to watch Cesario and Alice while sharing what she had overheard.

'I knew it—I told you how hard it is to keep your emotions out of things.' Her mother sighed. 'You haven't been married to Cesario for five minutes yet and you're already getting jealous and suspicious!'

Jess turned a hot guilty pink. 'Of course

I'm not! I'm only curious to know if what I heard is true.'

'So ignore the gossip and ask your bride-groom for the real story. If you don't make a major issue out of it, he'll probably be quite happy to tell you what really happened,' the older woman opined.

Jess knew that was sensible advice, but it was frustrating advice because she couldn't imagine questioning Cesario about something that personal. She returned to her seat at the top table and sipped her champagne, still longing for the real fizz of fun and optimism to magically infiltrate her bloodstream and lift her mood. Her boss, Charlie, came up to talk to her about the locum vet he had engaged to cover for her while she was in Italy. In the end, after much debate, she had not opted for a partnership at the practice, reluctant to own a rise in status that could only be attributable to Cesario's wealth and influence and concerned that such a move would only burden her with even more responsibility than she already had. Since there was only so much of her to go round, she had decided that working part-time would suit her changing circumstances better, allowing her to continue her career and keep abreast of new developments while allowing her more free time in which to meet Cesario's expectations and to work towards her ambition of having her animal sanctuary registered as a charity.

Charlie was moving away when a tall young man with dark curly hair approached her. She didn't remember him from the guest line-up and she was surprised when he asked her to dance, although she stood up with good grace.

'I don't think I remember meeting you earlier.'

'You won't. I've only just arrived with some friends for the evening party,' he told her cheerfully, reaching out a hand to clasp hers with relaxed courtesy. 'I'm Luke Dunn-Montgomery.'

He was a member of the family that had once owned Halston Hall. Jess felt her mouth fall open in surprise and she swiftly cloaked her gaze, although she could not resist subjecting him to one intense appraisal to satisfy her curiosity, for she knew by his name exactly whose son he was.

'Obviously, I know who you are,' Luke remarked once they were safely on the floor and the music had ground conveniently to a halt so that they could talk briefly. 'You're the cat that's not allowed out of the bag for fear that my father might lose votes for his youthful indiscretion with your mother...'

At that irreverent explanation for her birth father's refusal to acknowledge her existence, Jess lifted startled eyes to his. 'I didn't realise anyone else in your family even knew I existed.'

'I heard my parents arguing about you when I was a teenager,' he confided. 'My mother was furious when she found out that you existed.'

'I don't see why. I was born long before your parents married,' Jess pointed out tightly.

'Actually, they were dating at the time you were conceived,' Luke explained in a suitably lowered tone, his eyes dancing with rueful amusement. 'I was sworn to secrecy about you.'

'I didn't think I was that important,' Jess confided a touch bitterly when she cast her mind back to the cold reception she had received on the one and only occasion when she had tried to make the acquaintance of her birth father.

Currently a well-known member of parliament with a political career that meant a great deal to him, William Dunn-Montgomery had refused to have anything to do with the illegitimate daughter born to Sharon Martin while he was still a student. He had even had a solicitor's letter sent to Jess warning her to stay away from him and his family. It was as if she might be the carrier of some dread social disease, she recalled painfully. She marvelled that she had ever expected any warmer a welcome from the man when he had given her teenaged mother the cash to pay for an abortion and had then considered his responsibility discharged even after he learned that he had a daughter.

'I've always been madly curious about you—my only sibling,' Luke told her. 'My word, with that hair and those eyes you do look very like Dad's side of the family, although you're a little on the short side!'

At that quip, Jess glanced up at him, saw that he was tall and she grinned, her tension suddenly dissipating. He was her half-brother, after all, and she was pleased that he'd had the interest to attend her wedding and introduce himself to her. 'I didn't even know there were any Dunn-Montgomerys on the guest list.'

'Your bridegroom got to know my parents when he bought this place and my father's very proud of his extensive connections with the business world. I'm sure Father made a very polite excuse for his and Mother's non-attendance. I imagine he was very shocked when he realised who Cesario was marrying. It'll be a challenge for him to avoid you now.'

'Cesario doesn't know about my background,' Jess admitted. 'And I have no plans to tell him.'

'I can understand why you would prefer to keep quiet about my father.'

'Some secrets are better left buried. I don't see the point of treading on anyone's toes now.'

Luke took the hint and dropped the subject, walking her off the floor while happily answering all her questions. He had all the assurance of a much-loved only child and explained that, in the family tradition, he was a pupil barrister as his father and grandfather had been before him.

Cesario glanced over Alice's shoulder and saw Jessica with her tall male companion. His dark golden gaze zeroed in on his bride, noting the happy glow she exuded, and his eyes widened in surprise when she laughed, showing more animation than she had shown throughout the whole of her wedding day. That she liked the company she was in was obvious and he could see that she was chattering away. Cesario, who had never yet got his bride to chatter, stared and frowned, wondering who the young man was because he didn't recognise him.

Sharon intercepted her daughter to ask in a worried undertone, 'What were you talking about with Luke Dunn-Montgomery?'

Jess laughed. 'He knows about me and he couldn't have been friendlier.'

'His family won't like that,' her mother pronounced.

'That's not my problem,' Jess replied, reaching for another glass of champagne and registering that she felt remarkably buoyant.

'Watch out,' Sharon said anxiously nonetheless. 'It's safer not to get on the wrong side of people like that.'

'Times have changed, Mum. The Dunn-Montgomerys are not lords of the manor any more and the locals don't have to bow and curtsy when they pass by.'

And, at that moment, Luke reappeared at her elbow and insisted on being introduced to her mother before sweeping Jess off to meet his friends. The champagne had loosened her

tongue and made her more of a social animal
than usual. Luke's friends were fun and she
was giggling like mad over a silly joke when
Cesario approached their table, spoke to everyone with rather chilling dignity and anchored a hand that would not be denied to
Jess's elbow to raise her from her seat and
walk her away.

Bristling at that high-handed intervention,
Jess shot him a reproving look. 'What was
that all about?'

'It's time for us to bow out of the fes-
tivities.'

'But we aren't leaving for Italy until tomorrow morning,' Jess protested, realising belatedly as she glanced at her watch that time had
moved on without her awareness and that,
at what felt like very little warning, she was
about to embark on her much-agonised-over
wedding night.

'It's after midnight and our guests are beginning to leave, a fact that seems to have
passed you by while you were flirting—'

'I'm not Cinderella.' Jess froze, facial muscles tightening, slight shoulders stiffening as
Cesario herded her out to the magnificent
main staircase. 'And I wasn't flirting!'

'You've been flirting like mad with

Luke Dunn-Montgomery for the past hour!
*Maledizione*! I could hear you laughing across
the dance floor.'

On the wide first landing, Jess slung Cesario
a furious look and the truth trembled on her
lips, but she wouldn't let it loose. Why should
she admit that Luke was her half-brother and
that she was thrilled he had sought her out
and treated her like a sister? She didn't owe
Cesario any explanations. He might have
married her but he wasn't entitled to her
deepest secrets, particularly not the wounding or embarrassing ones. Cesario was from
an aristocratic privileged background similar
to her estranged birth father's and she cringed
at the thought of admitting that she was the
former squire's unacknowledged child by one
of the village girls. Even if it was the truth, it
sounded hideously, mortifyingly like something out of a nineteenth-century melodrama.
And when she was already struggling under
the humiliation of Robert Martin having been
responsible for the loss of Cesario's valuable
painting, and having had to admit to having
loan-shark, jailbird relatives as well, was it
really her duty to lower herself further in his
estimation?

'To be truthful it was good to have some-

thing to laugh about today!' Jess tossed back
cheekily, clutching the full skirts of her gown
in impatient hands as she mounted the stairs
and struggled to keep up with his long impatient stride. 'I've not been in much of a laughing mood recently.'

'Believe me, I've noticed!' With that ringing indictment, which any woman would have
taken as a direct criticism, Cesario thrust
wide the door of a big bedroom, furnished
with atmospheric pieces of antique oak and
a fire flickering in the grate to ward off the
chill of the late spring night air.

Jess stared wide-eyed and disorientated at
the room; she had never been upstairs in the
hall before. The Tudor magnificence of her
surroundings was in stark contrast to the contemporary décor that embellished the ground
floor reception rooms that she had seen.

'What's that supposed to mean?' Her tone
was truculent as she questioned his censori-
ous comment, but then she was assailed by
dizziness as her head began to swim. She
caught at the doorknob with her hand and
leant on it to steady herself on knees that
momentarily had all the consistency of jelly.
Perspiration broke out on her short upper lip
as she straightened up, wondering in dismay

if she might have been a little too free with the champagne cocktails on offer at Luke's table. Depending on how much she narrowed her eyes, the vast oak four-poster bed that dominated the room seemed to be shifting and changing position rather like a boat on the edge of a whirlpool.

'That, in spite of the fact that I've done everything possible to accommodate your needs, you have been a very sulky bride!' Cesario condemned, still picturing her glowing face as she sparkled as brightly as a Christmas tree ornament while she talked, giggled and smiled for that toyboy, Luke Dunn-Montgomery's, benefit.

'So, I'm human and imperfect and you're surprised at this discovery?' Jess fired back, stumbling slightly in her high heels as she moved away from the door. She pushed the door shut too hard and it slammed, very loudly, closed behind her, making him frown and wince. 'It isn't that easy to marry a stranger and contemplate living with him… although I guess with all the one-night stands you've had it will be no big deal for you!'

Indignation lanced through Cesario at that unnecessary comeback. He was not promiscuous and, although he was willing to acknowledge that he could be arrogant and demanding, he had made a genuine effort to make the terms of their marriage more attractive for her benefit. Not only had he arranged without her knowledge to have her six moth-eaten dogs microchipped and transported out to Italy for their honeymoon, he had controlled his aggressive instinct to intervene and call every shot. And he was very far from being impressed by the response that his generosity had so far won from her. 'You shouldn't believe the nonsense you read about me in the newspapers. I left one-night stands behind when I was a teenager.'

'What about Alice? When did you leave her behind?' Jess heard herself throw at him out of the blue, not even aware that she was about to hurl those nosy questions until the driven words emerged from her lips.

His ebony brows knit in excusable surprise at that sudden change of topic. 'Why are you asking about Alice?'

'I heard a couple of the guests talking…I understand that you and she were an item before she married your cousin.' Having opened the subject, Jess discovered that she could not make herself back off from it again. She wanted to know, she *needed* to know more.

'That's true.' His lean, darkly handsome features taking on a forbidding aspect, Cesario compressed his wide sensual mouth into a hard, inflexible line, his dark golden eyes screened. 'But it's not a good idea to listen to malicious gossip. The truth is that I put Alice through hell and it's a wonder that she stayed with me as long as she did. I didn't realise I loved her until she was gone and by then she was with Stefano and it was too late. I wouldn't have come between them. They're very happy together.'

As she listened Jess had slowly lost colour to pale and stiffen with discomfiture. She was horribly conscious that she had asked what she should not have asked and learned what she would sooner not have known. He had *loved* Alice, maybe still loved her, even though he couldn't have her. In fact, wasn't he exactly the sort of high-achieving Alpha male who would want a woman who was out of his reach all the more? He had stepped back and done the decent thing for Alice and Stefano's sake. It was not an explanation that pleased her or soothed her worries. But why did she have worries on that score? Why should it matter to her if Cesario was in love with a woman married to another man? That was none of her business. Their cold-blooded marriage, their *project*, was not based on emotional ties or expectations, she reminded herself ruefully. And if he was emotionally bonded to another woman, that could well be why he had decided that only the most practical of marriages would meet his requirements.

'I wasn't sulky today,' Jess fielded belatedly, lifting her skirts to kick off her shoes and sink her bare soles gratefully flat onto the Persian rug below her feet. At least that was what she intended to do but, somewhere in the midst of removing the second shoe, which necessitated her standing on one leg like a stork, she lost her balance and lurched sideways, knocking an occasional table and the floral arrangement on top of it flying in a noisy, tumbled heap.

'You were sulky and you've had too much to drink as well,' Cesario contradicted between gritted teeth of disdain, striding forward to haul her up out of the debris of dripping flower stalks and greenery while lifting the table back up with one impatient hand.

'Maybe I'm a little tipsy but I wasn't sulking,' Jess persisted in stubborn denial. 'If you knew me better you would know that I'm quite shy and not a chatterbox at the best of times. I don't like crowds much either and today has been a big strain.'

Cesario closed the distance between them and raked long brown impatient fingers through his cropped black hair, gazing down at her with a dark intensity that made her nerve endings pull taut with shockingly sexual awareness. 'I thought all women loved weddings?'

Her tummy performed a nervous somersault while the buds of her breasts swelled and lengthened. Hot-faced, Jess viewed him with huge silvery eyes. 'But I don't love you and now I'm in a bedroom alone with you and you're *expecting*—' Her voice cut off abruptly as though she had bitten back dangerously unguarded words rather than cause offence. 'Well, you're expecting what you've got every right to expect as a new husband and that's all I've been able to think about all day and—'

'I too, but not, I think, for the same reasons, *piccola mia*,' Cesario incised, his dark golden eyes hot and hungry on her tense oval face, his long, lean, powerful body taut as he swooped on the vase still leaking water and set it upright on the rug.

He closed a lean hand round her wrist to tug her closer. He felt the resistance in her slight frame and expelled his breath in a slow measured hiss. 'I don't want you when you're intoxicated and unwilling…'

So tense she could barely catch her breath, Jess gazed back at him and despised herself for playing that card when the flickering obstinate heat of arousal was shimmying through her pelvis like a mocking touch. In a movement that took him as much by surprise as it took her she shifted up against him, stretched up on tiptoe and pressed her soft mouth to his.

A masculine hand curved to her hip to crush her against him. Her heart thumping feverishly fast, she gasped as he drove his tongue between her lips in a delving, erotic assault that set up a jangling response throughout her entire susceptible body. Suddenly she wanted him more than she had ever wanted anything in her life and with a hot, sweet longing that came dangerously close to an edge of pain.

'There will be other nights,' Cesario quipped, lifting his handsome dark head, his dark eyes sardonic, and setting her back from him before walking to the door.

Trembling, senses awakened and cruelly crushed again, Jess studied the space where he had been and thought what a disastrous note she had chosen to begin their relationship on. *I don't want you when you're intoxicated and unwilling...* She cringed, despising herself for not being tougher. She had signed up for the marriage and cheating didn't come naturally to her. It didn't matter if Cesario loved Alice. It didn't even matter if he was convinced that Jess was a sulky, uptight bride and a flirt at her own wedding. They had had an agreement and she had just welched on the deal, and nobody could have been harder on Jess than she was on herself while she finally struggled free of her gown, washed off all her fancy make-up and climbed into the big bed alone. There she lay with her eyes wide open because whenever she tried to close them the room revolved behind her lowered eyelids in the most nauseating way...

# CHAPTER SIX

ALMOST unrecognisable in a stylish white linen skirt and top teamed with a bright turquoise jacket, sunglasses anchored firmly on her nose, Jess boarded Cesario's luxurious private jet in teeming rain the following afternoon. He had left the hall that morning to fit in a business meeting in the City before his departure.

Jess was still suffering from a hellish hangover and she had barely slept during the previous night. At some point during those slow-passing hours she had grudgingly acknowledged the truth of Cesario's criticism of her mood the day before. She had got the dream dress, the gorgeous groom and the fabulous ceremony, but she had not got the love, the caring or the happy-ever-after that brides looked forward to receiving. As a result, disillusionment and a horrid sense of being trapped had dogged her throughout her wedding day. It was as though the true cost of marrying Cesario di Silvestri had only really hit home after she and he had made their vows. But she had made an agreement with him and she would stick to it from here on in, she assured herself fiercely.

Cesario stepped onto the jet, his keen gaze shooting straight to the petite brunette seated in a comfortable tan leather upholstered seat. 'Jessica…'

Tensing, Jess looked up warily, worried about the reception she might receive after events the night before. 'Cesario…'

'I think we can do without the sunglasses,' he said wryly, with a nod in the direction of the rain streaming down the nearest porthole.

Jess breathed in deep and removed the tinted spectacles, knowing her eyelids were pink and puffy in spite of the make-up she had applied.

'And please let your hair down. I love your hair, *mia bella*,' Cesario confided as though that were the most normal thing in the world for him to say to her.

'It'll be a mess,' Jess warned him, pink warming her cheekbones. Wanting to match his generosity in not holding onto any spite, she reached up and dragged the band out of her hair so that her curls tumbled free to her shoulders. 'I couldn't be bothered to do anything at all with it today, which is why I put it up.'

At that frank admission a slanting grin curved his wide sensual mouth. He bent down and fluffed her mass of curls round her anxious face with gentle fingers. 'It doesn't need anything. It looks great just as it is,' he contended. 'I like the natural look.'

But Jess didn't think Cesario would recognise 'natural' unless it hit him in the face; he had probably never been exposed to the real thing. She suspected that more than one woman had gone to bed with Cesario fully made up and just as many had sneaked out of bed early the next day to 'brush up' before he got a first look at them. She had noticed the very high levels of grooming amongst the female wedding guests and had appreciated that just to pass muster in such company she would have to make much more effort than she was accustomed to with her appearance.

'About last night,' she began awkwardly.

'Forget about it. Today we start again—

fresh page, open book,' Cesario pronounced smoothly, sinking down in the seat opposite her and buckling up for the take-off. She found herself covertly watching his every fluid movement. The smooth bronzed planes of his high cheekbones framed his straight, strong nose and the sensual perfection of his full-modelled mouth. By the time his lashes lifted to reveal his dark golden eyes as he tilted back his dark head to address the stewardess, Jess was staring helplessly: he was a heartstoppingly handsome man.

'Tell me about where we're going,' she urged, keen to find out about their destination and talk to him for a change.

'Collina Verde…it means "Green Hill". It's the country house where I spent my earliest years with my mother. It's in the hills above Pisa and very beautiful,' he murmured softly.

Jess recalled him telling her that he had grown up without a mother and scolded herself for having made no attempt to learn more about his background. After all, it was on the basis of such little nuggets of information that most relationships were built and life would be easier for both of them if she made the effort to be more interested. 'What happened to your mother?'

Cesario compressed his lips, his dark eyes taking on a grim light. 'She died from an overdose when I was seven years old.'

Jess was taken aback by that uncompromising admission. 'That is so sad. It must've been very hard for you to handle that loss at such a young age.'

'I blamed my father. He had had a string of affairs and they were living apart by then,' Cesario mused wryly. 'But he had a great line in self-justification: he said it was in the blood and that I would be exactly the same.'

Jess was too craven and too tactful to dare to comment on that issue. 'What was it like for you when you had to live with your father instead?' she asked curiously.

His dark eyes gleamed like polished bronze and he gave her a wry half-smile. '*Dio mio*. He wasn't cut out to be a family man any more than he was fit to be a husband. He resented being tied down. He was very competitive with me and it got worse as he aged and had to face that his youth was gone. Nothing I achieved was ever quite good enough.'

In recognising that he came from a much less happy and secure background than her own, Jess had plenty to think about during that flight. After a light early supper they landed in Pisa at the Galileo Galilei airport. Though it was by now early evening, it was a good deal warmer than it had been in London and the sun was still shining by the time the waiting limousine wafted them in air-conditioned comfort deep into the Tuscan landscape. She had expected lovely countryside but she sank into another dimension of appreciation entirely at her first glimpse of the most distant rolling hills and the serried green ranks of the grapevines, softened here and there by the silvery clouds of foliage that distinguished the olive groves. All the buildings, fashioned of pale apricot-coloured stone, seemed ancient and the medieval towns and villages on the hilltops were impossibly picturesque.

Collina Verde sat on top of a hill ringed by woodland, and although its sheer size made it imposing it was a less formal property than she had expected. A fortified farmhouse composed of several rambling buildings, it sat with its castellated roof below a blue and gold evening sky and enjoyed the most breathtakingly timeless view she had ever seen. She got out of the car, still entranced by the outlook of the mountains and the valley below, and enjoyed the light breeze that lifted her hair back from her brow and cooled her warm skin.

'It is lovely,' she remarked, and then a chorus of familiar barks sounded and she jerked round in disbelief to see her six dogs pelting frantically across the paved courtyard towards her in noisy welcome. 'My goodness, how on earth did they get here?' Her attention flipped to Cesario. 'You arranged this?' she queried in visible disbelief.

'With the help of your mother. I know you planned to leave them behind with your rescue animals and I'm sure they would have been well looked after but I know how attached to them you are,' Cesario advanced, considering himself to be well rewarded by the shining look of appreciation etched in her face.

'I'm just…stunned!' Jess confided, hunkering down to be engulfed in a wave of wet noses, scrabbling paws and noisy greetings.

Cesario had suspected that the white outfit would have a limited shelf life with his bride and his worst expectations were fully met by the time Jess straightened again to head for the front door, her pack of dogs prancing round her. Her skirt had acquired dusty paw prints and damp patches and her top was speckled with dog hairs but she gave him a huge smile that let him know that, while the designer wardrobe worth many thousands had failed to impress, his gesture in flying her pets out to Italy had won him his highest yet approval rating.

'I mean, I know you're not a doggy person,' Jess pointed out breathlessly. 'Which is why it was such a particularly kind and thoughtful thing to do—'

'And not what you expect from me, *piccola mia*?' Cesario completed silkily.

'Well, no, it wasn't,' Jess agreed without hesitation. 'But I was wrong.'

Cesario was honest enough to feel a shade guilty, for all he had done was issue instructions to his staff, who had taken care of all the official hassle required to transport the dogs abroad on pet passports.

'Hugs gets so upset when he doesn't see me,' Jess explained, fondling the nervous wolfhound's ears while it gazed up at her adoringly. 'And Magic gets frustrated when he can't communicate.'

Cesario frowned, studying the Scottish terrier currently playing dead on the ground with four paws stiffly extended so that his tummy could be tickled. 'How does he communicate?'

'He's deaf and the man I hired to look after the sanctuary didn't know any doggy sign language,' she proffered, making a signal with one hand that made the terrier roll over and sit up, his little black beady eyes pinned to her.

Cesario was impressed by the demonstration. 'I've never really had a pet. My father disliked animals,' he told her, curving a hand to her elbow to walk her into the house. 'The closest I ever came to it was having a horse.'

They stepped over the greyhound, already fast asleep in the lengthening shadows cast by the wall. Weed, the thin grey lurcher, pushed his long narrow face into Cesario's hand and Jess stared in surprise. 'My goodness, Weed must like you. Someone once treated him badly and he rarely approaches anyone for attention.'

Resisting the urge to snap his fingers in dismissal of such notice, Cesario entered his Italian home with Weed sticking as close to him as a shadow. His housekeeper, Agostina, welcomed them all indoors, and as soon as introductions were over Jess surrendered to curiosity and wandered straight off alone for a tour. It was an atmospheric house, gently aged and respected and full of charm. Worn terracotta tiles that gleamed stretched underfoot, while wooden ceilings vaulted above big airy rooms furnished with light and colourful drapes, comfortable sofas and plain pieces of solid country furniture. A series of tall narrow doors stood wide open onto a terrace overlooking the valley and a table and chairs sat in the inviting shade of a big chestnut tree.

Pausing only to instruct the dogs to stay and not to follow her, Jess headed up the stairs. Their luggage had been parked in two different rooms, she noted, unsure whether she was pleased or not with the boundary that was being acknowledged. Business, not pleasure, she told herself resolutely, but it was an unfortunate thought, for she did not like to think that her body had anything to do with a business agreement. Seeking a distraction, she peered into the first of a set of magnificent marble bathrooms fitted out in opulent contemporary style. She took off her jacket and walked out onto a wrought iron balcony to enjoy the view.

'You will have to be careful not to get

sunburned in this climate,' Cesario remarked, making her jump, for she had not heard his approach.

Jess swivelled round. 'It's an absolutely gorgeous house,' she told him with enthusiasm.

An indolent smile curved his darkly handsome lips. 'I'm glad we can agree on that. I had it updated last year and it is the perfect spot for a honeymoon.'

The colour of awareness flickered into her cheeks and he stretched out lean brown hands to clasp both of hers and ease her closer.

'Honeymoon...honeymoon...honeymoon,' he rhymed teasingly. 'It doesn't take much to make you blush, *moglie mia*.'

The setting sun cast still-heated rays on her skin, but not as hot and overwhelming as the hungry seal of his mouth over hers in a passionate kiss. The world went into a tailspin as the slow pulsating throb of arousal travelled all the way through her responsive body. Her nerve endings leapt, making every inch of her deliciously sensitive, so that even the hand he smoothed across the swell of her bottom was a source of pleasure and her legs shook beneath her.

His broad chest rising and falling and his breathing fractured, Cesario gazed down at her rapt face, his dark eyes smouldering hot gold. 'I won't take anything for granted with you—yes or no?'

And Jess liked that he had still thought to ask the question. He was tugging her indoors out of the fading light and she blinked, long lashes sliding almost languorously up on her light grey eyes and there was no hint of reluctance there. Desire had dug unshakeable little talon claws into her, vanquishing the fear and uncertainty. Her body wanted to connect with his again and strain towards that distant source of satisfaction she sensed.

'Yes,' she told him shakily.

'*Sì*...your very first word in Italian, *moglie mia*.'

'*Sì*...but tell me what you are calling me,' she demanded as he drew her back to the bed.

'My wife,' Cesario translated with assurance, 'which you are.'

For some unfathomable reason, that was the first time Jess felt truly married. Those words achieved what the pomp and ceremony of the wedding day had not. She smiled, allowing herself to enjoy the warm hum of arousal in her pelvis. She refused to think about her scars, telling herself instead that

most people had things they disliked about
their bodies and that she was no different.
So, she stood quiescent while he removed the
linen top to reveal a pretty white and blue bra
and then she moved forward and began without hesitation to unbutton his shirt. Her hands
grew a little less dexterous as the edges of the
shirt fell open to reveal the hair-roughened
bronzed flesh beneath.

In acknowledgement of that wave of shyness, Cesario tipped up her chin and crushed
her raspberry-tinted mouth below his again,
revelling in the sweet strength of her response
and the way her fingers dug hard into his
muscular shoulders. He kissed her and then
he kissed her again, skilfully tasting the vo-
luptuous curve of her lips and the honeyed
secret corners of her tender mouth and still
he wanted more, wanted everything she had
to give with a raw edge to his hunger that
was refreshingly new to him. She trembled
against him, enslaved by the sexual probe of
his tongue darting inside her mouth and the
urgent masculine erection she recognised
when his hand closed to her hip to crush her
against his big powerful frame. Her whole
body rejoiced in the effect she was having
on him.

As he released the zip on her skirt and it pooled round her feet Cesario lifted her clear of its folds and brought her down on the big wide divan bed crisply dressed in linen. Before he removed his hand he brushed the roughness of the skin on her back and he glanced down in surprise at the long pale scar there.

'Did you have surgery there?' he asked.

Jess froze and angled away from him to present him with a defensive spine, only now his attention was fully engaged and he saw the furrow of scar tissue marring the pale skin and he touched it with his finger.

'*Per l'amor di Dio,*' Cesario exclaimed in surprise. 'What the hell happened to you?'

Jess flipped back to him and lay flat. She pressed two fingers to the final scar on her midriff and said fiercely, 'You missed one!'

Cesario focused on that final pale line cruelly bisecting her creamy skin. 'Those must surely have been life-threatening injuries?' he breathed starkly, black brows pleated as he studied her with questioning dark eyes that for once had no gleam of mockery.

'A…knife attack while I was at university. I almost bled to death,' Jess responded jerkily, and then she folded her lips closed and stared at him and in the depths of her pale glittering eyes he saw her fear that he would persist in his questions.

Cesario contrived to shrug a broad shoulder as though he saw knife wounds on his lovers every day and he half turned away to remove his shirt and kick off his shoes. His expressive gaze was veiled to conceal the true strength of his reaction from her because he was enraged by the image of her being slashed by a knife and helpless. She was so small, so feminine, but maybe those traits had made her a more appealing target, he reflected with grim cynicism.

'Sorry, I just don't like to talk about it,' she said unevenly, one hand curling into a fist on the sheet as if even saying that much was a major challenge. 'Maybe I should've warned you—I know my scars are ugly…'

Having shed his trousers, Cesario came down on the bed beside her and bent his tousled dark head to the scar on her abdomen. Her heart hammered with tension, butterflies fluttering loose in her tummy as he pressed his mouth gently to the slightly puckered skin. 'Not ugly, just part of you. I'm sorry you suffered an experience like that and I certainly didn't need warning, *piccola mia.*'

He was rarely at a loss for the right thing to say, she thought enviously, only half convinced by his words and gesture that he was not repelled, but the worst of her tension had evaporated. The ferocious tightness of her muscles eased and she rested her head back on the pillow and breathed again. 'You see, I'm really not a perfect doll.'

'You're talking to a guy who wanted you even when you sported a dirty waxed jacket, muddy boots and a team of misfit dogs,' Cesario reminded her lazily.

'I'm surprised you didn't have the dogs booked into the local beauty spa for some grooming,' Jess teased, balancing on her elbows to stretch up and tilt her parted lips in invitation as though a piece of elastic were pulling her to him to rediscover that warm, sexy mouth of his for herself again.

And that next kiss ravished and seduced and left her dizzy and breathless, wondering where he had been all her life, for no other man had ever made her feel that way. She was already finding out that Cesario was not the guy she had believed him to be. He had much greater depth than she had ever been willing to concede when she reflected on their often spiky exchanges in the stable yard. She had

repeatedly failed to look beyond the rich sophisticated façade to the male beneath that
glossy patina of worldly success.

Her bra melted away during the kissing
and, while he palmed the small pert mound of
her breasts, he stroked her pointed nipples and
captured them between his lips and sucked
until the tingling buds were hard and swollen. Until then, she had not known that she
might be so sensitive there. He caressed her
until she was gasping for breath and a pool
of liquid warmth had infiltrated her pelvis.

'I want this to be really special for you,'
Cesario husked. 'But it might hurt.'

'So, get it over with,' she urged appre-
hensively.

Cesario gave her a wicked grin that
squeezed her heart inside her chest. 'Shame
on you—that's the wrong attitude to take. A
good lover never rushes a woman.'

He tugged up her legs and skimmed off the
white and blue matching knickers, sliding a
hand between her slender thighs to find the
engorged bud below the black curls on her
mound. He teased her with the ball of his
thumb and her hips rose off the bed in sensual
shock at the sweet erotic surge of arousal. It
was almost too intense for her to bear and she

was hugely conscious of the surge of moisture there.

Cesario pulled back from her and she studied him with sensually lowered eyelids, taking in the hard sleek contours of his broad chest and the muscles flexing across his flat stomach as he leant back and removed his boxers. He was magnificent and more than a little daunting to inexperienced eyes. He pulled her back to him and studied her with a hint of amusement in his beautiful eyes. 'I promise to be gentle,' he intoned, carrying her hand down to his bold shaft and encouraging her to explore his dimensions.

Her hand closed round him, for she was full of desire and curiosity, and she learned that he was strong and smooth, velvet over steel. Answering heat flowered between her legs so that when he took her mouth again with hungry urgency she more than reciprocated the feeling. He began to explore her most secret and responsive flesh, tracing the delicate folds, teasing the nub of her desire and then the damp little entrance. It wasn't long before little whimpers of sound were escaping her throat, the strength of her wanting making her legs tremble while the unbearable craving and the ache at the heart of her grew stronger

by the second. She had not known that anything could feel that powerful and least of all
that it might be him who introduced her to
the powerfully addictive force of desire.

He taught her to want what she had never
learned to want, only wondered about, what
she had truly believed she might go to her
grave without experiencing, and she had honestly thought that it wouldn't matter because
she wasn't really missing anything important.
So he taught her differently, stroking her with
skilful fingers, licking at the wildly sensitive
buds of her nipples while he surely, gently
prepared her for the ultimate pleasure. But the
yearning inside her for more steadily grew in-
tolerable, sharp-edged, greedy and impatient
so that she bit in impatient reproach at his
lower lip and let her trembling fingers close
tight into his luxuriant black hair.

Fluid and strong, he came over her, sliding
between her thighs when she was shaking
and desperate with pent-up need. She was
wildly eager for that first gentle thrust, feeling the stretch of her inner tissue struggling
to contain him and then the surge of his hips
against her as he drove deeper. It hurt a little
more than she had expected and she could not
suppress a cry of pain. Instantly he stopped,

gazing down at her with those drowningly dark and golden eyes of his that were so beautiful they made her ache.

'I'm sorry, *moglie mia*,' he whispered, brushing her tumbled curls from her brow to press a benediction of a kiss there. 'It will ease…I hope.'

Her inner muscles tightened round him and he groaned with an uninhibited sensuality that thrilled her and he shifted lightly, slowly, sinking into her by erotic degrees until she didn't know where he ended and she began. But it was an overpoweringly good feeling and she moved sinuously beneath him, angling up her hips to encourage him, all discomfort forgotten. As he withdrew and came back into her, her excitement began to build. Excitement laced with deep, deep pleasure at the motion of him in her and over her. His slow, steady rhythm ensured that the tight feeling low in her pelvis began to expand and spread outward, sucking her into a vortex of intense driving sensation. And then without even knowing where she was going and simply blindly allowing the force of her response to carry her with it, she reached a peak and the incredible waves of pleasure gathered her up and threw her down again on the other side. In a daze she floated back to earth again.

Cesario was watching her with dark, dark eyes when she recovered her senses again and his hand was closed over one of hers, his body hot and damp and intimately masculine against her thigh. She looked back at him with light eyes that still reflected some of her wonderment at what had just transpired. His strong jaw line squared.

'Don't look at me like that. Don't forget our agreement,' he breathed suddenly, his keen gaze narrowed on her feverishly flushed face. 'I didn't ask for your love and I don't want it. We will share a bed, nothing more, until a child is born, *piccola mia*.'

It was like an unanticipated slap in the face for Jess and she went straight into shock, recognising that he, of all men, would recognise when a woman might be getting a little too attached, a little too serious. Her facial muscles tightened, her expression carefully schooled to blankness as a wave of anger and pain broke inside her like a tide crashing on the shore. She would not give him the satisfaction of knowing that he had hit pay-dirt with that cold-blooded warning. She would not respond with the angry resentment that would reveal that he had wounded her.

'I don't have love to give you,' Jess fielded flatly as she deliberately shifted away from him, rejecting that deceptive togetherness for the pretence that it so clearly was. 'I love my family and my pets and some day I will love my child, but I'm afraid that's it. I am a very sensible person when it comes to my emotions.'

A slight darkening of skin tone over his cheekbones hinted that she might have touched him on the raw. He screened his gaze and murmured levelly, 'I just don't want you to be hurt.'

'I'm strong, much stronger than you seem to think,' Jess countered, and then, in a tone of polite enquiry calculated to underline that declaration for his benefit, 'Are you staying here for the night? Or do we sleep separately?'

Cesario sat up as though she had elbowed him in the ribs. 'My room is next door.'

'Goodnight,' Jess told him sweetly.

*'Buone notte, ben dorme…*sleep well,' he breathed, springing out of the bed, pausing only to pick up his clothes before he vanished through the connecting door.

Sleep well? Jess might almost have laughed at that piece of advice until she cried. She freshened up with a shower in the superb adjoining bathroom, went downstairs briefly to take care of her dogs and then finally crawled back into bed, the slight persistent ache at the very heart of her as much a reminder of what had changed in her life as the lingering scent of his cologne and his body on the pillow beside hers. Breathing that aroma in, she groaned out loud and shut him out of her head.

Her thoughts came in a kind of vague shorthand because she was blocking out so much of what she was feeling and denying the pained sense of loneliness, loss and rejection she was experiencing. Her husband had introduced her to sex. He was good at sex and she was very lucky that that was so, she told herself determinedly. He had tried to pretend that theirs was a normal marriage but he had lied. He didn't want her to care about him. But she was a proud and clever woman and she would respect his warning. She would not make the foolish mistake of falling in love with a man who'd made it clear from the outset that he could never love her back…

She also wondered dully if it was true that

he was still in love with Alice. That would give him a very good reason to make a marriage of convenience in an effort to produce the heir he required to gain legal title to his family home. If he was already in love with another woman, a businesslike arrangement was his only real hope.

Jess told herself that it made no odds to her whether or not Cesario loved another woman. Such subtleties, such secrets, were beyond her remit and immaterial in terms of a marriage already openly acknowledged to be one of pure practicality. Why should she give a hoot if he cherished another woman in his heart? On that challenging thought, sheer mental and physical exhaustion dragged Jess down into a deep, dreamless sleep…

# CHAPTER SEVEN

CESARIO was suffering from an appalling headache. He had taken his medication but it had yet to kick in. Actually, he wanted a drink, but knew that alcohol was a bad idea with powerful painkillers. He massaged his brow and tried to loosen his taut neck muscles while studiously endeavouring to suppress all the negative thoughts threatening his equilibrium. He had been warned about headaches and this was as bad as he had been promised: so far, so normal…

He knew his bride thought that he was a cold, callous bastard, but he had said what he'd had to say and drawn a necessary line in the sand. He didn't want her on his conscience. He didn't want to hurt her either. It struck him as strange that he had not foreseen that possibility *before* he married her. Was he really so single-minded and selfish that he had not considered the damage he might inflict? Evidently, he was.

Determined to stay grounded, he reminded himself that the marriage was a project, a business agreement and little more. His bride might seem vulnerable and naïve, but it would be unwise to overlook the fact that he had paid a fat price for her services when he accepted the loss of that painting and dropped the chance to prosecute her father. And obviously he wanted Jessica to find pleasure in his bed, since it might well take months for a conception to take place. The big seduction scene that he had unintentionally staged could only have been motivated by subconscious common sense, he reasoned grimly. It was then that he got himself the stiff drink he knew he shouldn't have and still lay awake until dawn broke the skies.

The following morning Jessica awoke to the chink of china rattling and sat up to be served breakfast in bed on a tray complete with a linen napkin and a pretty flower in a bud vase. So, *this* was what it was like to be spoiled, she thought ruefully, pushing her wild tumble of black curls out of her eyes as the smiling maid chattering in broken English opened the curtains and threw open the doors onto the balcony, inviting in fresh air and sunshine. Jess discovered that she was ravenous and she washed down pancakes and fresh fruit with juice and cappuccino coffee.

A slim figure in floral shorts and an emerald green T-shirt, her black curls bouncing on her shoulders, she descended the stairs. A door stood open wide onto a rear courtyard and, with a hail of excited barks and yelps, her doggy posse came charging through it. All her pets, with the exception of Weed, were present, and as she straightened from her greeting session Cesario appeared in a doorway, Weed lurking shyly to one side of him.

Self-conscious, Jess tensed and tried not to stare but it was a tough challenge. Cesario was less formally clad than she had ever seen him, in a casual shirt that clung to his wide shoulders and powerful chest and linen trousers that accentuated the long muscular strength of his legs and the lean tautness of his hips. But while informal it was still cutting-edge Italian designer style he sported, and his ruffled black hair and the shadow of stubble round his handsome mouth only roughened the edges of his usual perfect grooming to ensure that he looked even more masculine and sexy than he normally did.

Her mouth ran dry, the colour in her cheeks heightening as she briefly relived the intensity of her pleasure with him the night before and her tummy flipped, her legs trembling below her.

'Where have you been, Weed?' she asked her stray pet, concentrating her attention on him because it was safer than focusing too much on the sleek predator by his side.

'He just wandered in and went to sleep under my desk,' Cesario told her with a shrug that disclaimed all responsibility for the development.

'My goodness, you start work early! I'd better go and feed the dogs…'

'They've already been fed. I employ a dog handler in my security team and he's been taking care of the practicalities.'

Taken aback by that assurance, Jess gave him a disarmingly natural grin. 'I can't get over the novelty of having people do things for me—I mean, breakfast in bed, what a treat!'

'Every day can be a treat for you now,' Cesario murmured, enchanted against his will by that sudden flashing smile that lit up her oval face. During the night he had thought about the knife attack she had mentioned. Belatedly recalling what had surely been a defensive wound on her hand, he had wanted to know the whole story, but he was reluctant to risk traumatising her by asking her to satisfy his curiosity. She had said she might have died and then he would *never* have known her. His lean strong face shadowed as he forced that gloomy thought out.

'No, I don't like being spoiled. I'm not helpless and I'm too used to doing things for myself,' Jess fielded briskly, suddenly wanting and needing to hold onto what was familiar lest her life become subsumed entirely by his.

'You're on your honeymoon.'

Her nose wrinkled. 'Call it a holiday, not a honeymoon. By no stretch of the imagination could we be like a honeymoon couple,' she pointed out drily.

'What I said last night wasn't meant to offend you,' Cesario drawled. 'It was intended to—'

'Save you the hassle of dealing with a lovesick bride who wants to hang onto you a few months down the road?' Jess trilled quick as a flash. 'Relax, that's not going to happen.

I'll be looking forward to getting my freedom and my own life back.'

For a split second Cesario looked as though he might have been about to argue with that assessment, but then he closed his handsome mouth, watching her with screened liquid dark eyes that gave away nothing. Jess, however, had few illusions about the warning she had received the night before. The very fact she was still a virgin had probably given him commitment-phobia. She was, after all, dealing with a man accustomed to women who fell madly in love with him and his lifestyle and then were reluctant to let go of him and the luxury again. But she had no intention of becoming one of that undistinguished crowd. Jess had fought many a fight against poor odds in her life and had emerged triumphant. There was nothing of the loser in her genes. Hopefully she would walk away from Cesario di Silvestri with a child, but only because that was her choice as well as his, she told herself fiercely.

'So, how do we spend the first day of this holiday?' Jess enquired brightly.

Cesario slung her a wicked grin full of sexuality and fantasy, his dark golden eyes dancing with amusement, and hot pink drenched her cheeks.

'Okay…' Jess conceded between gritted teeth. 'But in between times I want to see Tuscany.'

'Your wish is my command, *delizia mia*.'

*'Again?'* Cesario husked as a slim hand wandered across his hair-roughened thigh with an intent he knew all too well only to discover that he was ahead of her and already primed and ready for another bout of lovemaking. Being with a woman who wanted him as much as he wanted her, he had discovered as the days of their honeymoon had unfolded, was a very invigorating experience.

This particular day, though, had started off on a purely cultural note with a trip to the beguiling hilltop town of San Gimignano, dominated by its thirteen medieval towers. Cool as a spring flower in a pale blue skirt and white lace top, Jess had admired the Ghirlandaio frescoes in the Renaissance chapel of Santa Fina and she had succumbed to highly infectious giggles when Cesario compared her profile to one on the wall. They had enjoyed a leisurely lunch in a thirteenth-century town house followed by vintage wine served in the piazza. There, slowly but surely, intelligent conversation had faltered as their eyes had met and other rather more basic instincts had taken over.

But it was Jess who had taken Cesario by surprise when she had ultimately leant across the table to whisper feverishly, 'Get us a room...'

They had barely made it through the door of the airy tower room of a nearby hotel he had hurriedly taken for them before, still almost fully clothed, they were enjoying each other up against the wall with a scorching raw-edged passion that Cesario had never before dared to unleash on a woman. The looks they had shared in the piazza over the wine had acted as the most arousing session of foreplay he had ever experienced. Even now, lying naked and bronzed in a tangle of sheets, he was still reliving the hot, tight, wet seal of her body round his and the gasping sounds of unashamed pleasure that had rung in his ears even as she tried to stifle them for fear of being overheard. He had already had her three times and he knew it would not be the last time that day. As those delicate fingers of hers enclosed his bold erection and she lowered her luscious mouth to caress him,

Cesario just lay back and closed his eyes, literally drunk on pleasure. Being married was turning out to be a whole lot more enthralling than he had ever dared to hope.

Jess loved to plunge Cesario into that rich well of sensuality where she held sway. It was a power-play, a runaway triumph for a woman who had been a virgin a mere six weeks earlier and pretty ignorant of what it took to be an equal bed partner. But that aside, touching Cesario, making love with Cesario, just *being* with Cesario was also the biggest source of pleasure Jess had ever known. Telling herself that it should not be that way hadn't worked as a defence against feeling things she knew she shouldn't be feeling with him. Only in the realm of sex and physical expression could she let her barriers down, freely showering him with the physical hunger he ignited and sealing her mouth and her mind shut on the thoughts and the emotions that accompanied the desire.

Sharon Martin had spoken wisely when she'd warned her daughter that it wouldn't be easy to live with a man without her emotions getting involved. But Jess didn't blame herself for failing to maintain her defences, she blamed Cesario for transforming himself into the perfect new husband, a fabulous lover and all-round fantastic companion, whom pretty much any woman would have found irresistible.

In the aftermath of yet another session of hot, satisfying sex, Jess lay with her heart racing and her body aching in the circle of Cesario's arms. He was still holding her, stroking her spine, his mouth gently brushing her temples. He was doing that fake caring thing again and part of her wanted to slap him for it. She had tumbled headlong in love with him but she still had her brain and she didn't need the pretences, didn't want them. It was just sex they shared and she could handle that reality—she had never been a coward when it came to the hard realities of life!

'Sex with you sizzles every time,' Cesario told her appreciatively. 'You could make me monogamous.'

Her grey eyes flashed silver and she lifted her head. 'If I thought for one minute that you would stray while I was still living with you, I would probably kill you!' she swore shakily, passion betraying her.

Cesario stretched back against the pillows with predatory grace and no small amount of male satisfaction at what he took as a compliment. 'I do believe you would, *moglie mia*. You're not the sort of woman any man would dare to take for granted.'

'I'm not a proper wife…don't talk as though I am!' Jess warned him waspishly. 'A proper wife wouldn't drag you off to a bedroom in the middle of the day and shag you half to death…'

Cesario shifted again and grinned wickedly like the cat who'd got the cream while he curved a strong arm round her to hold her close. 'The wife of my dreams certainly would…'

'I'm not the wife of your dreams either.' Her fingers spreading defensively across his hair-roughened pectorals as she lay against him, Jess could hear the flat note in her delivery and prayed that he couldn't.

Jess was fully convinced that Alice, the beautiful American former fashion model married to Stefano, would have been the true wife of Cesario's dreams. Alice and Stefano and their two gorgeous little boys lived only a few miles away from Collina Verde and they were regular visitors. While the men had happily talked politics, business and the intricacies of producing award-winning wines, Jess and Alice had got to know each other.

Jess genuinely liked Alice and admired her talent as an amateur artist. But she was also always painfully aware of Alice's extensive list of appealing traits. Alice was gentle and kind, a shining example of a woman who was as lovely on the inside as she was on the outside, and Jess was convinced that no man who had lost a woman of Alice's worth could have easily recovered from the experience and moved on. She was not surprised that Cesario had once loved Alice or that Alice and Cesario remained very close. Jess had yet to see anything she could object to in their behaviour but in their presence she was always conscious of how well they knew each other and of how new her own relationship with Cesario truly was. It was a struggle not to be jealous of his bond with the other woman.

As Jess shifted her hand down to his flat, hard stomach Cesario closed his fingers over hers and his thumb smoothed gently and consideringly over the scar on her hand, his lean, powerful body tensing in response. 'Tell me who did this to you,' he urged tautly. 'I need to know what happened to you.'

After a moment of silence, Jess slowly released her breath in a rueful sigh. 'I attracted the attentions of a stalker in my first year at university. An unemployed loner whom, as far as I know, I'd never actually met or even spoken to,' she explained reluctantly. 'When the police showed me his photo after the attack it was a challenge to even recognise him—'

'A stalker?' Cesario was already frowning. 'I assumed you'd been the victim of some random robbery.'

'There was nothing random about it and no theft involved. I began getting cards and little gifts in my accommodation mailbox and I had no idea who they were from. At first I actually thought it was romantic…all that love-from-afar-stuff girls hear about!' she breathed with sudden bitterness.

His arm tightened its grip. 'You weren't to know it was an abnormal interest.'

'Well, I found out soon enough when my stalker saw me out and about with a male friend he assumed to be a boyfriend. That's when his interest took a creepy turn: the cards turned abusive, calling me a whore…and a slut…and a whole lot of other *dirty*…' Jess was trembling and her voice was shaking.

'It must've been very frightening for you.' Cesario wrapped both his arms securely round her slight body to comfort her and tugged her into full contact with him. 'Clearly he had problems. Did you go to the police?'

'The cards didn't threaten me with violence, so he wasn't committing an offence. The law's been changed since, but back then a woman had very little protection from that sort of thing,' Jess told him heavily. 'I got really scared because it was obvious that he was spying on me. But hardly anyone saw him as a serious threat. In fact my friends tried to make a joke about his fixation on me. One evening I came back from class to the flat I shared, laden with books and shopping...'

'And he was waiting for you?' Cesario prompted darkly, his nostrils flaring.

Jess was pale but the words were flowing more freely now. 'He just appeared round the corner of the landing and there was something weird about the way he looked at me. I just *knew* it had to be him and I ran back to the stairs. I dropped my bags but I wasn't quick enough. When I saw the knife I put up my hands to protect my face and I don't remember anything else but screaming. A neighbour came out and interrupted him and my attacker fled. He ran out into the road and got hit by a car. He died...he died and I wasn't sorry,' she admitted sickly. 'But I would have lived in fear for ever more if he had survived.'

Cesario held her until the deep trembling slivering through her slim frame had subsided and she was breathing evenly again. 'I'm sorry you had such a terrifying experience. I just needed to know what had happened,' he volunteered wryly. 'But I understand now why you've always played down your looks...'

'After the attack I just couldn't be comfortable wearing clothes that might attract male attention. Before that I was a normal teenager and I wore miniskirts and all the rest of it,' Jess admitted ruefully. 'It's not that I think every man might have it in him to be violent, it's more the way a woman's looks can encourage a man to objectify her and see the outside without seeing that there's a real living, breathing, feeling person underneath.'

'I've been guilty of that miscalculation many times, *bella mia*,' Cesario admitted with a grimace as he acknowledged the fact.

Jess lifted her curly head to send him a significant look that brought a frown to his lean, hard-boned face. 'I should think so too with your reputation.'

'If you're basing your opinion on what's been printed about me, keep in mind that the

British press only began depicting me as a wild, promiscuous playboy after I dared to dump their darling, Gilly Carlton.'

His reference to one of the most popular soap stars on British television made her raise her brows. 'I didn't even know that you and she—'

'We didn't—she was always drunk. A couple of casual dates and I'd had enough of her falling out of chairs, cars and doorways!'

'But my opinion of you wasn't formed by anything I read in the newspapers,' Jess confided, giving him a deliberately mysterious glance that was pure provocation. 'To be honest, I had a source of information much closer to home.'

'Who?'

'I'm not telling.' Throwing back the sheet, Jess pulled playfully free of his hold and slid off the bed. 'Just for once I'm going to grab the first shower.'

'I'm feeling lazy. We could stay here tonight, dine out and go home tomorrow. It is our last week.'

'I would love that.' Padding into the compact en suite bathroom, Jess was ridiculously pleased that he appeared to be as aware as she was that their honeymoon idyll was almost at an end. It touched her that he was keen to make the most of what time was left.

If she had not known that they had married simply to conceive a child, she would have described the last six weeks they had shared as a magical time of discovery and joy. As it was, she knew she had to keep her feet firmly pinned on the ground and pour cold water on her more fanciful thoughts and reactions for, within days, she would be returning to England, her job and usual routine. And since she was beginning to suspect that she might already have conceived she was wondering just how much she could hope to see of Cesario in the future.

Did he too suspect that she might have conceived? Had he noticed that her menstrual cycle had not once kicked in since they'd became lovers? Surely he must have noticed even though he hadn't said anything? Perhaps she should visit the local doctor when they got back to Collina Verde. Could it have happened so fast? Her face warmed as she towelled herself dry and stood back to allow him access to the shower. They had had sex a lot. Some days they had barely got out of bed. And even now she could hardly keep her hands off him. It shocked her how much she craved him, how often they could make love and for how little time that fierce hot arrow of desire would remain satisfied. So, it was not beyond the bounds of belief that she might already have fallen pregnant. She was excited and apprehensive—excited at the prospect of a baby, but apprehensive that conception would mean the end of all intimacy between her and Cesario. After all, once a baby was officially on the way, their 'project' would be complete and there would no longer be a reason for them even to live below the same roof.

From the bedroom window, she looked out over the textured terracotta roofs that lent such warmth and colour to the panoramic view of the old town as the medieval houses beneath them stepped down the hillside. Her memory served up cherished images of the relationship they had created between them. He had bought her a gilded image of a saint in the market at Castelnuovo di Garfagnana, which he had insisted reminded him of her. She thought the resemblance was in his imagination alone. Possibly that was the first thing he had said and done that he should *not* have in the first forty eight hours of their stay in

Italy, she mused unhappily. There was no room for such frills and fancies in a practical marriage of convenience.

But then there had been very little practical about the experiences they had shared. In the tour of Tuscany that Cesario had treated her to, he had walked hand in hand with her like a lover through winding streets and alleyways, happy to shop in tiny traditional workshops and sample the freshest of food in the picturesque restaurants. The same male who had warned her not to fall in love with him had moved the goalposts without telling her and she had been afraid to remark on it lest it change the wonderful ambience between them. They'd had picnics amongst the wildflowers on deserted hillsides and long chatty romantic evening meals on the elegant loggia at the house listening to the classical music she loved. She had adored Florence and Siena, but had found both cities too hot and crowded at this time of year and he had promised to bring her back once the height of the tourist season had passed. Now, she wondered if he would ever keep that promise.

She had learned that he was human too, once she came to appreciate that he occasionally suffered from shockingly bad migraines, which he flatly refused to talk about. Indeed he seemed to look on any admission of feeling unwell as the behaviour of a wimp and his ridiculous stoicism brought a tender smile of remembered amusement to her lips. Somewhere along the line, she acknowledged ruefully, their holiday had turned into a proper honeymoon.

He had bought her a fabulous designer bag in Florence and a painting that she found so ugly she had threatened to dump it while he believed it would grow on her and refine what he saw as her unsophisticated taste in art. And then there was the jewellery…he really loved to give her jewellery and to see her wear it. Her fingers touched the delicate choker of golden leaves that curved round her throat like an elegant question mark. He had bought it for her thirty-first birthday, which he had remembered without any prompting from her. He had also insisted that she had to have a diamond pendant and earrings if she was not to look only half dressed beside Alice when they dined out with the other couple.

He had shown her Etruscan tombs and magnificent palazzos and taught her to distinguish a good wine from an indifferent one. He had laughed when she'd told him that she had not known what cutlery to use on that disastrous first dinner date and she'd had to explain how intimidating she had found that because, born into wealth and fine dining as a way of life, Cesario had not initially understood the problem.

She had fallen in love with her husband and did not know how she could possibly have *avoided* doing so, because Cesario di Silvestri had somehow succeeded in making himself indispensable to her comfort and happiness.

Over dinner that evening, Cesario was still demanding that she name her mole concerning his reputation and she finally took pity on him and confided that her parents lived next door to his former housekeeper.

Cesario frowned. 'She signed a confidentiality agreement. All my staff have to. I can't believe she's gossiping about my private life…'

Jess winced. 'I should have kept quiet and I probably shouldn't have listened either. Dot does seem to cherish a certain resentment over being put into retirement before she was ready to go.'

'Because an audit revealed that she was helping herself to the household cash and selling off wine on the sly,' Cesario chipped in drily. 'That's why she was put out to grass and Tommaso was brought in.'

Jess was shocked by that explanation. 'But you didn't prosecute her?'

'She's quite an age and had worked for the Dunn-Montgomery family all her life. Rather than make an example of her in my role as the new owner of the Halston estate, I thought it best to just write it off to experience and replace her.'

They walked hand in hand back to the little hotel. Three quarters of the way across the moonlit piazza he paused and kissed her with a slow, deep hunger that made her heart crash against her breastbone.

'I misjudged you,' she confided in a guilty rush. 'I believed all the bad stuff. I thought the very worst of you from the moment we met.'

Cesario looked down at her in the moonlight, dark eyes gleaming above classic high cheekbones. 'But you don't now.'

'Are you a love cheat like the tabloids say?' Jess asked abruptly, allowing her need to know free access to her deepest insecurities.

Cesario groaned out loud in dismay at that blunt query. 'Is my answer going to be held against me?'

'Probably,' Jess declared.

'I did cheat sometimes when I was younger and sex was still a game, but even then I didn't lie about it or make promises I couldn't keep,' Cesario answered. 'Growing up with my father, who always had more than one woman on the go, I saw the cost of that kind of deception time and time again. I've never wanted to live my life the same way. Screaming rows, jealous scenes and bitter break-ups are better avoided.'

'Deception is the one thing I couldn't forgive,' Jess confessed. 'Honesty is incredibly important to me.'

Cesario screened his gaze, his lean, strong face hollowed by unmistakeable tension. Glancing up at him in the small hotel foyer, she surmised that she had got too serious and made him feel uncomfortable. Were her standards of behaviour too high for him? It was an unsettling suspicion. Perhaps he even suspected that she was trying to get him to make her promises and the notion brought colour to her cheeks, for she wanted nothing from him that he did not choose to give her of his own accord.

Long after Cesario went to sleep that night,

Jess lay awake by his side and wondered what their future held. Or even how far that fragile future might extend in front of her.

# CHAPTER EIGHT

A DAY and a half later, on the eve of her return to England, Jess stared down in consternation at a pregnancy test wand and its indisputable result.

There it was, ironically, the outcome she had secretly come to fear most. Seemingly it had taken hardly any time at all for Cesario to get her pregnant and it was a discovery that ripped Jess into emotional shreds and plunged her into violent conflict with herself. She hadn't expected to conceive so quickly and had simply assumed that it would take at least a year. One half of Jess wanted to get up and dance round the room and tell everyone and anyone who was willing to listen that she was expecting her first child. For so long she had dreamt of becoming a mother and now the opportunity had finally come her way and she knew that she ought to be feeling ecstatic.

But the other half of Jess was cast into complete turmoil by the positive result. Would this result mean that her marriage to Cesario was now effectively over? Confronted by that threatening fear, it was impossible for her to be ecstatic or even accepting. She loved Cesario, she was not yet ready to lose him, could not see when she would ever be ready to. Would she now be returning to Halston Hall alone, there to wait out the course of her pregnancy with nothing more than occasional phone calls from the man who had fathered her child? In the circumstances, how much more involved could she expect Cesario to be in her life? The whole point of their marriage had been to conceive a child, she reminded herself bleakly. He would not have married her otherwise. Now that the baby had become reality Cesario would be free to return to his former lifestyle of wine, women and song, a possibility that made Jess feel quite sick with apprehension.

Of course, it was perfectly feasible that the result was wrong, Jess began to reason frantically, surveying the discarded packaging and deciding all of a sudden that it looked like a cheap and unreliable testing kit. Her bowed shoulders began to rise again. She just knew that Cesario wouldn't be overly impressed by the news that she had run her own test. She really would need to see a doctor to get a proper diagnosis and it would be much simpler just to wait until she got back to England where she could easily make an appointment at the village surgery. Her frown of worry ebbed. It would be crazy to burn all her boats at once, so she would keep the unconfirmed result of the test to herself until she had irreproachable proof of her condition, she decided, her spirits recovering from their temporary dive into the doldrums. She really couldn't be *too* cautious. Wouldn't it be dreadful to tell Cesario that she was pregnant and then discover that she had made a ghastly mistake?

Of course, in the short term, she would be careful to take every possible precaution with her health in case she did receive a positive confirmation, Jess reflected. At the very least she would stay off alcohol and be careful of what she ate. To date, however, she was feeling her normal healthy self. Admittedly she was tiring a little more quickly than usual, but that tiredness and the tenderness of her breasts were the only physical changes she had noted and nothing she couldn't live with. Torn in two by her conflicting feelings, she rested a hand against her still-flat belly and wondered if there really was a baby growing in her womb.

Attired in a simply cut crimson dress that flattered her slender curves with a close fit, Jess went downstairs for lunch. Agostina, their housekeeper, mentioned that Alice was with Cesario. Jess was about to go in the rambling main reception area to join them when she was startled to hear Cesario exclaim angrily, 'No! That's out of the question!'

'But I can hardly meet her eyes as it is,' Alice was arguing in a tone of distress. 'Jess deserves to know the truth, Cesario. How is she going to feel if you don't tell her?'

Round a corner and hidden from the view of her husband and his companion, Jess was frozen to the spot by the dialogue she had almost interrupted. Now her imagination was flying free and she was eavesdropping, wanting and desperately needing to know what they were talking about that had got both of them so worked up.

'What Jess doesn't know won't hurt her. It's

a fallacy that the truth is always preferable or kinder.'

'But I feel so guilty whenever I'm with her—'

'You won't be with her again for quite some time. We're leaving for England tomorrow morning—'

'It doesn't matter how you wrap it up. What we're doing is wrong,' Alice argued emotively. 'She's being cheated!'

'I refuse to discuss this with you any more, Alice,' Cesario cut in with icy finality.

*What we're doing is wrong. She's being cheated.* Oh, my goodness, *Oh. My. Goodness!* Jess thought sickly as she stumbled blindly back to the hall and headed like a homing pigeon for the stairs again to take cover in privacy. They were having an affair behind her back and Alice was feeling guilty? Alice, it seemed, actually wanted to come clean about the affair, but Cesario was all for keeping their adultery a secret. Of course, he had excellent reasons for wanting to keep quiet, didn't he?

Had he owed her such an honest explanation of where his heart really lay when they first embarked on their marriage of convenience? Possibly not, for fidelity and deeper emotions had not featured in what she had innocently believed that marriage would entail. What was in his heart had been nothing to do with her when he had only married her to ensure that any child they conceived was born within wedlock. And he still needed a child to ensure he could inherit Collina Verde, so naturally he wouldn't want Alice to rock the boat with ill-judged confessions of unfaithfulness just at this moment.

It all made perfect sense to Jess and she felt dizzy and sick with shock and disillusionment. She dropped down on the edge of the bed. Her skin was clammy and her tummy was on a nauseous roll. On every level of her being she was appalled by what she had just discovered because she had expected better of the man she had married. For a start, Cesario and Stefano were as close as brothers. Both were only children and had grown up together; Cesario, in particular, had spent a lot of time with Stefano's family following his mother's premature death. Jess would have sworn that Cesario was deeply attached to his cousin, and that Stefano was a doting husband who would be devastated to find out that the wife he adored was sleeping with his best friend. How could Cesario betray Stefano like that? Jess called herself a fool, a blind, trusting fool, for not being more suspicious of a woman who, having once been Cesario's lover, still remained on such openly warm terms with him. How often were such continuing friendships purely platonic? And Alice was an extremely beautiful woman...

Jess squeezed her eyes tight shut and knotted her fists. Maybe she should not have been so quick to dismiss the daunting tabloid reports of Cesario's sexual exploits and heartless nature. Having fallen in love with him, she had wanted only to think good things of him and had happily assumed such rumours to be lies couched to entertain readers who enjoyed being shocked by the shameless shenanigans of the rich and famous. Cesario had certainly misled her, so it was hardly surprising that he had also misled his cousin into believing that his relationship with Alice was innocent.

Jess asked herself what she did now. As the saying went, she was neither fish nor fowl and really had no idea what her status was as Cesario's wife. Was he currently sleeping with Alice? Or was that intimacy being reserved for when his relationship with Jess ended? Or was she kidding herself in thinking that the lovers might be practising that kind of respectful restraint? At the same time, Jess had spent almost every waking hour with Cesario since their wedding and she could not think when Alice and Cesario could have had the opportunity to cheat. He had enjoyed no un-explained absences or trips anywhere and had never failed to answer his mobile phone when she had called him; if he was having an affair with Alice it was an incredibly discreet one and he was being unbelievably careful not to rouse suspicions. Was it possible that there was another explanation for the mysterious conversational exchange she had overheard?

Wondering if she was being silly even to think that she might be mistaken, Jess went back downstairs. Cesario entered the dining room at almost the same time.

'Isn't Alice joining us?' Jess asked, to let him know that she was aware of the other woman's visit.

Cesario gave her a level look that carried not a shred of discomfiture. 'No. I asked her to stay but she has guests arriving this after-noon for the weekend. Before I forget, she left a gift for you. I believe it's a belated birth-day present,' he advanced, striding out of the room and reappearing a minute later with a package, which he extended.

Jess frowned. 'What is it?'

'I think she's painted something for you,' Cesario said carelessly.

Jess removed the wrapping paper and the bubble-wrap beneath and found she was looking at a very charming framed drawing of her dogs lying in a group on the shaded loggia. She did recall Alice sketching out there one day but had simply assumed that she was drawing the magnificent view. 'It's really beautiful,' she remarked in shock at the generosity of the gift, noting how Alice had carefully managed to capture the traits of each animal. 'She's very talented.'

'You're much more impressed with that than you were with the painting I bought you,' Cesario noted with an incredulous lift of his expressive ebony brows.

Jess studied the delightful drawing of her pets, which she would cherish, and guilty discomfiture engulfed her. She could not credit that the woman who had taken the time and effort to give her such a well-chosen, personalised present could, at the same time, be having an affair with her husband. Did that make her foolish and naive? However, now Jess could not believe that Alice was capable of such dishonesty while simultaneously behaving like a caring, considerate friend. She had no idea what Alice had been arguing with Cesario about, but she was increasingly convinced it could not relate to the two of them being involved in a secret affair. Was it possible that she herself was guilty of being just a little bit paranoid about Cesario? Was she more jealous of his bond with Alice than she had any reason to be? Seemingly she had leapt far too fast to the wrong conclusion and envy was the most likely cause. Her face warmed at the idea.

'You're very quiet this afternoon, *piccola mia*.'

'It's very hot. I'm kind of sleepy,' Jess said truthfully.

'You do look tired. But then I never leave you to sleep the night through in peace,' Cesario remarked with a rueful hint of discomfiture. 'But tonight I will—'

'No, you won't,' Jess objected before she could even think about the bold statement she was making when she disagreed. 'I'll have a nap now.'

A potent sexy grin curled Cesario's mouth at that offer, his lean dark features reflecting his amusement. 'I like being in demand very much, *moglie mia*.'

But if he knew she might already be pregnant, would he still want to be in demand? Or would he suddenly appreciate that all his options were open again and that the intimate phase of their marriage was over and done with? In spite of those misgivings, Jess fell asleep within minutes of lying down on the bed in the shaded bedroom and she slept the afternoon and early evening away.

When she got up again, she tracked Cesario down in the room he used as an office. Glancing up, he saw her hovering in the doorway, bright as a butterfly in a lilac top and skirt. 'Come and see this,' he urged with a frown.

Jess wandered over and stared down at the sheet of paper he was poring over. 'What is it?' she prompted uncertainly.

'Rigo sent a scan of it to me this afternoon.'

Jess stared down at the sheet of paper. Jumbled letters cut from a newspaper had been put together to form a note. But the spelling was so appalling that it was hard to work out the words, although she was quick to register that it had been put together in English. 'Where did this come from? And who is Rigo?'

'Rigo Castello looks after my security and

the original of this communication arrived at Halston Hall this morning. It's offering to return my stolen painting for a finder's fee…'

'Your painting…the one that was stolen? A *finder's* fee?' Jess exclaimed in disbelieving repetition.

'I think we can safely assume that the thieves sent this demand,' Cesario contended, his hard, handsome face sardonic. 'Presumably they have found it impossible to sell the painting for the kind of money they were hoping to receive and are now hoping to ransom it back to me.'

Jess was still struggling to decipher the jumble of misspelt words on the sheet. Helpfully, Cesario read it out, right down to the concluding assurance that further instructions would follow as to where the money was to be left. 'What on earth are you going to do?' she muttered in bemusement.

'Well, I'm not going to pay for the return of my stolen property,' Cesario declared with derision. 'I refuse to be held to ransom by criminals!'

Jess shifted uneasily where she stood, all too well aware that he might well have got his art work back had he been able to approach the police, but of course that would incriminate her father in the robbery. She was beginning to feel very uncomfortable because adolescent memories were also stirring and it was impossible to forget the mortifying involvement of her mother's relatives in the crime. At that instant she was one hundred per cent convinced that she knew exactly who was responsible for the theft of Cesario's painting.

'When I was a teenager, my cousins, Jason and Mark, once sent a letter like this to intimidate a neighbour who had complained to the police about them,' she told him ruefully. 'The spelling in the letter was dreadful. I think this could be from them and that they must have your painting.'

Cesario surveyed her with hooded eyes. 'I must say that I have married into a very interesting family.'

Her face flamed. 'Look, don't make a joke of it. Think of how you would feel if you were related to people like that!' she urged.

'You're right, *moglie mia*. That was a cheap crack and undeserved, particularly when you've just given me useful information. We will not discuss this again,' he completed, his strong jaw line clenching.

'I'm sorry about the painting. I know how much you valued it,' she said awkwardly.

His lean, darkly handsome features softened. 'It's not your fault and I don't hold you responsible in any way. Don't blame yourself because your father got in over his head and did something stupid.'

Jess felt that that was a generous response in the circumstances and she had cause to remind herself of that during the hours that followed. Over dinner Cesario seemed preoccupied and he excused himself to catch up with work afterwards and did not join her in bed that night. It was the first time in weeks that she had slept alone. She lay awake thinking about their return to England in the morning while trying not to wonder if Cesario was keeping his distance because he was repulsed by her thieving relatives. It was all very well for him to tell her that she was not to blame, but she could not forget that she was only married to him and possibly even carrying his child because of that robbery.

In the morning, Jess could hardly keep her eyes open and she made more use of makeup than she usually did in an effort to lift her wan appearance. She did not see Cesario until after breakfast and he still seemed distant.

Determined not to waste any time in finding out whether or not she was pregnant, she phoned to make an appointment to see her GP in Charlbury St Helen's before they even left for the airport and caught their flight home to the UK. Her dogs would already be at Halston Hall waiting to greet them.

'This is your home now, *piccola mia*,' Cesario pronounced as the limo drove through the turreted gates of the Elizabethan property. 'Make whatever changes you please to the house. I want you to be comfortable here.'

It was a generous invitation and it warmed her uneasy heart and steadied her nerves about the future, until it occurred to her that Cesario had made no such open-handed comments in relation to his other homes round the world. Collina Verde in Italy, it seemed, had been her home only for the honeymoon. She tried hard not to read any significance into that fact. If Cesario was rather cool in her radius it was probably only the natural result of the robbery fiasco, because when the thieves had offered to sell his own painting back to him they had undoubtedly added insult to injury.

'By the way, I've bought you a new vehicle to get about in,' Cesario informed her as they travelled down the drive to the hall. 'Your car was ready for the scrap heap.'

'But I don't need a new car!' Jess protested.

'There it is—the blue one parked out front,' Cesario informed her as smoothly as if she hadn't spoken.

It was a brand-new, top-of-the-range Range Rover, ten times more expensive then her elderly four-wheel drive and embellished with the most sumptuous cream leather upholstery Jess had ever seen. 'I gather this is part of my new swanky image,' she said tartly, turning her head to look at him after she had walked all the way round the luxury car.

'No, not in this case. I didn't think that wreck you were driving was very safe and I didn't want it breaking down and stranding you somewhere lonely late at night,' Cesario contradicted silkily, making her feel ungracious.

Jess was on the brink of protest about his interference until she registered that she actually liked the fact that he was concerned about her safety. It was a satisfyingly husbandly concern and allowed her to feel more like a real wife than she usually dared to feel. 'It's not going to look clean and perfect for very long with me and the dogs using it,' she warned him ruefully.

As Tommaso appeared beaming at the front door a canine flood surged out to acknowledge their arrival with a flurry of barks and scrabbling paws. Cesario strode off towards the garages after telling Jess that he had an urgent appointment to keep. Weed raced round the corner in his wake—the skinny lurcher, whose confidence had grown by leaps and bounds in Italy, had become her husband's shadow, and Magic bounced along after them.

Jess changed into more comfortable clothing and went out to keep her medical appointment at the local surgery. Thirty minutes later she had the confirmation she had sought and, feeling somewhat shaken by the news that she would have a child by the following spring, she went to visit her mother.

'Cesario called in an hour ago,' Sharon Martin told her daughter when she arrived. 'He spoke to your father at work and then came here to ask me some questions about your uncle Sam.'

Jess fell still and grimaced at that information. 'What's he up to?'

'Your husband wants his painting back and

he's determined to get it,' her mother confided ruefully. 'He told your father that he would try to keep him out of things but that he can't guarantee it—'

'That's not fair!' Jess gasped in consternation. 'I have an agreement with Cesario…'

'And he wants the agreement *and* he wants his painting back. Typical man,' Sharon Martin quipped. 'He wants it all and sees no reason why he shouldn't have it.'

Jess breathed in deep. 'You're going to be a grandmother again next year.'

Initially taken aback by the change of subject, her mother stared at her and then, with an exclamation of pleasure, she rushed forward and gave her daughter a warm hug. 'My goodness, that didn't take long! Are you pleased?'

Squashing her doubts and insecurities about Cesario and keen to ensure that her mother didn't worry about her, Jess fixed a smile to her lips. 'I'm over the moon! I haven't told Cesario yet, so keep my secret for me.'

Before returning to the hall, Jess called in at the veterinary surgery to check the work rotas. She went straight to talk to her boss because her pregnancy would mean there had to be a good deal of reorganisation at the practice. She would have to take extra safety precautions and consider the kind of jobs she took on. She thought it said a lot for Charlie that, even after taking all that approaching hassle into account, he was still able to offer her his hearty congratulations and happily reminisce about his early days as a new father.

When she got back to Halston Hall, Tommaso was in the hall supervising the placement of a very large canvas of what looked like a desiccated tree twisting in a storm. Rigo Castello, a heavily built older man, was poised nearby wearing a large approving smile. Jess gaped at the painting and recognised it at once from Cesario's description of it. She asked where Cesario was and raced breathlessly into his office with her dogs accompanying her. 'You got it back? How on earth did you do it?'

Cesario straightened his long, lean, powerful body fluidly from his lounging position on the edge of the desk and made a hand signal to Magic, which made the deaf and excitable terrier sit down and stop barking. 'Your Uncle Sam is a sensible man.'

And then without any warning at all, and as if someone had suddenly pulled a rug from beneath him, Cesario lurched sideways and crumpled down into a heap on the floor. 'Tommaso!' Jess shouted in shock, dropping to her knees by Cesario's side and noting that he was ashen-faced, with perspiration gleaming on his brow.

His security chief, Rigo, joined her first. 'Let me deal with this, *signora*.'

'I'll call the doctor!' Jess exclaimed because Cesario appeared to be unconscious.

'That won't be necessary, *signora*. Mr di Silvestri is already coming round.'

Jess watched Cesario's lashes lift on dazed dark golden eyes. He blinked several times. Her heart was pounding with adrenalin inside her ribcage. Rigo addressed his employer in rapid low-pitched Italian and, raking a trembling hand through his cropped black hair, Cesario responded.

'I'll call the doctor,' Jess said again.

'No—I don't want a doctor!' Cesario asserted with what struck her as quite unnecessary force. As he struggled to get up she noticed that he leant heavily on Rigo's arm.

Jess was concerned enough to argue with her husband. 'You're obviously not well! You need to see a doctor…'

'I tripped on the corner of the rug and I

must've struck my head,' Cesario countered, dismissing Rigo, who shot him a troubled look before leaving the room.

Her brow indented as she glanced at the rug, which seemed to be lying perfectly flat. She had only seen him fall and it had looked more like a collapse or a faint to her than a moment of clumsy inattention. Not only did his interpretation not make sense, she could think of no reason why he should lie about it. She studied him worriedly, grateful to see that he had regained colour and looked more like himself. It shook her to recall that just months ago he had meant very little more to her than a stranger in the street, while now he meant the whole world to her.

'You said you had spoken to my uncle?' she prompted, her curiosity about the painting overtaking her concern now that he seemed to have made a recovery.

'Yes, and he didn't want any trouble. He was even less keen on the idea of the police being called in. He told me that if his sons had my painting he'd have it back here within the hour and presumably they did,' Cesario pointed out drily.

'You intended to bring in the police if you didn't get anywhere with him?' she pressed.

'Rather than let your cousins get away with robbing me blind? *Yes*,' Cesario confirmed without hesitation, his lean strong face stamped with resolve. 'I warned your father but, fortunately for him, I've got my property back and the matter can be forgotten about now.'

'Well, I'm glad you got it back but you didn't really play fair, did you?' Jess commented, light grey eyes full of reproach. 'To keep my father safe, I married you and agreed to give you a child, which was a pretty tall order. But in spite of that, today you were ready to sacrifice my father.'

'Why worry about what didn't happen, *piccola mia*?' Closing the distance between them, Cesario spread his long fingers either side of her anxious face and gently smoothed her skin in a soothing gesture. 'Your father is innocent of any criminal intention and he was not at risk. I accepted that after speaking to him personally following the robbery and if the police had got involved they would have reached the same conclusion that I did, *moglie mia*.'

Jess trembled, more affected than she was prepared to admit by his proximity and words of understanding. He'd called her 'my wife' and instantly everything seemed lighter and brighter. She wrapped her arms round his neck and within seconds he was kissing her with a hot, driving hunger that left her dizzy with its intensity. Her body quickened, desire rising embarrassingly fast so that she pushed against his hard, muscular frame, her breath ragged in her throat, her nipples tight and throbbing.

'Bed,' Cesario muttered thickly, grasping her hand and urging her out of the room and up the stairs.

'It's time for dinner,' she muttered.

'*Non c'è problema!* Tommaso won't let us starve, *bellezza mia.*'

And the hunger he roused in her with his second kiss was fierce and relentless, every plunge of his tongue sending a responsive quiver through her slight body. It was as if there were a flame desperate for fuel burning at the heart of her as she hauled off his jacket and pulled open his shirt. He laughed softly and then crushed her mouth almost savagely beneath his. As he removed her clothes with impatient hands she knew that, somehow, the same overwhelming urgency and need for fulfilment was driving him.

He sank into her hot, wet sheath hard and

fast and released a groan of pleasure that acted like an aphrodisiac on her. She felt wild as she craved every thrust of his lean, muscular hips, her body jolting and straining towards a climax even while he paused to savour the moment. She came apart in the circle of his arms, ravished by the exquisite pleasure that washed through her in a sweet drowning tide, so that even afterwards all she was conscious of was the race of his heartbeat against her breast and the damp, reassuring solidity of his big powerful body against hers.

'I've never needed anyone the way I just needed you, *cara mia*,' Cesario framed heavily, both arms wrapped round her as though he was still reluctant to let her go.

And in the fading light she smiled and touched a loving hand to his shadowed jaw line, admiring his fabulous bone structure and the inky darkness of the long lashes that framed his bronzed eyes. She loved to be needed, lived to be needed by him, and his passion for her made her feel special. It would have been the perfect moment to tell him that she was pregnant but she was quick to discard the idea, preferring to concentrate on their togetherness rather than on an announcement that might well bring their current living arrangements to an end. She would share her news in the morning instead, she decided, and she stayed silent, even though they later got out of bed to enjoy a late dinner.

What remained of the night was long, since they made love until dawn. Cesario was tireless and his hunger for her seemed both ravenous and unquenchable. When exhaustion finally overcame her, she slept deeply and wakened to find that she was alone. She had planned to make her announcement over breakfast with Cesario but the morning was already well advanced.

Clad in cropped trousers and a silk top, she hurried across the imposing landing of the mansion that was now her home and sped downstairs. She found Cesario in his office talking in Italian on the phone. Weed and Magic were curled up together below his desk. Eyes tender with love, she watched Cesario unnoticed from the doorway for the space of minute, revelling in the memory of the closeness they had shared and proud of the intimate ache that was the penalty for such passion…

# CHAPTER NINE

'JESSICA…' Cesario perceptibly tensed the instant he saw her there, his lean strong face pulling taut and shuttering. 'I'll be with you in a moment.'

A little hurt by the reserve she sensed in him, Jess asked Tommaso to bring them coffee and took a seat. 'I've got something to tell you,' she said as soon as Cesario had finished his phone call.

Tommaso created a welcome hiatus with his return with a tray and Cesario wandered over to the window with his cup cradled in one lean hand, sunshine glinting over his black hair and adding reflected light to his charismatic dark eyes. 'What is it?' he asked casually.

Jess lifted her head high. 'I'm pregnant,' she told him quietly.

Cesario looked revealingly stunned, as

though that was the last piece of news he had expected to hear. His ebony brows pleated in a questioning frown. 'You can't be…'

'I am.' A confident smile of achievement illuminated her face. 'I saw the doctor yesterday and had it confirmed, so there's no mistake.'

'But so soon, so, er, *quickly*?' Cesario breathed in stilted English, his surprise still lingering in spite of her explanation. 'We're both in our thirties and I believed it might take months.'

'No. We'll be parents by the end of January next year,' Jess told him excitedly, wanting to infect him with some of her enthusiasm because he was standing there so still and quiet.

'January next year,' Cesario repeated slowly.

She thought he looked pale beneath his bronzed skin and more like a man who had been dealt a severe shock than a man given news he should have been eager to hear. His strong facial bones were clearly defined, his brilliant eyes hooded so that she had not the slightest idea what he might be thinking. It was the most complete non-reaction that she had ever experienced and very far from what she had hoped to receive.

'You're not pleased,' she breathed unevenly.

Cesario unfroze and took a hasty step towards her, only to come to a halt again and then hover with uncharacteristic uncertainty. 'Of course, I'm pleased!'

Jess could feel herself turning stiff and defensive, for any hint of the warm intimacy of the night hours had been well and truly scuppered by his attitude. 'No, you're not pleased and I don't understand why you're not. Isn't this what you wanted? Didn't you marry me so that I could give you a child?' she prompted, her voice getting more shrill without her meaning it to, and for a horror-stricken instant she was afraid she sounded whiny.

'*Che cosa hai*…what's the matter with you?' Cesario chided, pulling her resistant body to him with firm hands. 'Does falling pregnant make a woman shockingly cross, *bellezza mia*?'

'No, of course, it doesn't!' she rebutted tightly, gazing up into his breathtakingly handsome features with bewildered eyes. 'It's the way you're behaving that's making me feel like this. You've changed your mind, haven't you? You don't want a baby any more!'

Cesario closed his larger hands firmly over

hers. 'I have never heard such nonsense. If you are having my baby—'

'I *am*,' Jess slotted in truculently.

'Then naturally I am overjoyed, *piccola mia*,' Cesario insisted, his beautiful dark eyes intent on her troubled face as if he was willing her to believe what he was telling her. 'But I am very concerned that I should hear this wonderful news and then have to tell you that, owing to a business emergency, I have to fly to Milan this afternoon and leave you alone here.'

Although her heart sank at the prospect of him leaving and she could barely credit that he should already be returning to Italy when they had only left the country the day before, she was relieved by his clarification. Her cherished announcement had clearly suffered from bad timing when he was already preoccupied with business problems and his imminent departure.

'I'll be absolutely fine here. My family are within reach if I need company. But, to be frank, I have a good number of hours to catch up at work and I'll be very busy as well.'

His hold on her hands tightened. 'Now that you're carrying a baby you'll have to rest more.'

'I'll be sensible. I am only contracted to work part-time now,' she reminded him. 'I also need to get the accommodation here and staffing sorted out for my rescue animals. I've got plenty to do while you're away.'

And she maintained that upbeat outlook until he took his leave a couple of hours later. The last impression she wanted him to leave with was that of her being irritable and difficult. But even as she set off for work wearing sensible clothing and driving her opulent new car with her dogs confined behind a special screen in the boot area, she was conscious that, no matter how she looked at it, Cesario's response to the news of their baby had still fallen very far short of her fondest hopes.

Jess was convinced that Cesario had not been pleased. Something had altered since their marriage. Had he changed his mind about having a child with her? Admittedly she had conceived more easily and quickly than either of them had expected and he had been unprepared for her announcement. But could that simple fact have caused him to have second thoughts about fatherhood? She kept on picturing his expression at the instant she had given him her news. He had looked bleak, disturbed…*guilty*? Her brow furrowed.

From where had she received the impression
that he felt guilty? That had to be her imagination because why on earth would he feel
guilty about her having fallen pregnant just
as he had planned?

Over the next four days Jess was exceptionally busy both at work and at the sanctuary.
She received an influx of unwanted dogs from
the council dog pound. People often surrendered pets because they weren't allowed to
keep them in rental accommodation and, these
days, more and more because they couldn't
afford to feed them or cover veterinary care.
Cesario rang her twice, brief, uninformative
calls that might have come from an acquaintance rather than a husband. Jess tormented
herself with recollections of the reality that
theirs was not a real marriage and never had
been and maybe only now was she seeing
proper evidence of the fact. Possibly the passionate nature of their relationship had blurred
the boundaries and confused them both, only
Cesario did not appear confused any more,
she acknowledged unhappily. Cesario now
seemed to be putting more than physical distance between them because he was treating
her with detached and impersonal formal-
ity. She felt as if she was losing him and it

unnerved her, for intelligence warned her that she had never had a normal claim to him. He had never loved her and lust was not an advantage now that she was carrying his baby.

On the sixth day after his departure, the estate manager called up to the hall to ask her to get in touch with Cesario on his behalf as he was having trouble reaching him. Jess could not get an answer on Cesario's mobile phone, which went automatically to his messaging service, and finally she rang his head office in London, only to be told by his PA that he had taken a few days off and would not be back at work until the start of the following week.

'Is he still in Milan?' Jess pressed.

'Mr di Silvestri is in London, *signora*,' the woman responded in audible surprise. 'I'll let him know that you want to speak to him.'

Jess was shaken. Cesario had allowed her to believe that he was in Italy when he was actually in *London*? Her heart sank at that awareness because she could not think of an innocent explanation for such behaviour on his part.

'There's no need for you to contact Cesario now. I'll see my husband before he receives any message you could give him.' Frowning,

Jess replaced the receiver and then she used her mobile to try and contact Alice. The other woman's phone also went straight to voicemail and when she called the landline at Stefano and Alice's Italian home she was told that Alice was visiting friends in England.

For the second time in the space of two weeks, Jess was eaten alive by cruel and wounding suspicions. Fear flung her mind wide open to the worst possibilities. *Was* Cesario having an affair with Alice? Were her husband and his former girlfriend together in London? The sheer gut-wrenching pain of that apprehension ripped through Jess and suddenly she could not bear not knowing the truth. Blinking back tears she couldn't hold back, she decided that she would go to London immediately, visit Cesario's apartment and confront whatever she found there head-on. Would she find him there with Alice? She *had* to know what was going on. How could she live otherwise? How could she even get out of bed tomorrow if she didn't know whether or not their marriage was still alive?

Although Jess was aware that Cesario owned an apartment in London, she had not previously had a reason to visit it. She drove to the local station and caught the city-bound train, thinking it was ironic that she felt nauseous for the very first time during that journey. Her emotional state of mind seemed to be seeking a physical outlet. She took a taxi to an ultra-modern apartment building and travelled up in the lift, squinting at herself in the reflective steel walls, wondering if she could possibly be as pale and miserable as she looked.

Rigo Castello let her into the apartment and there was no sign of reluctance or discomfiture on his part, which warned Jess straight off that she was not about to surprise Cesario *in flagrante delicto*. Straightening her spine and throwing back her stiff shoulders, she told herself that she had every right to ask awkward questions of the father of her unborn child before she walked into the airy reception room with splendid views over the city.

Cesario was outside on the rooftop terrace, striding towards the sliding doors that were wide open at the far end of the room. His black hair was blowing back from his lean, darkly handsome face. Unusually he was not wearing a business suit, but jeans and a black T-shirt that enhanced the sculpted lines of his lean, muscular body. He did not seem surprised by her sudden appearance, a reality that led her to assume that his PA had given him prior knowledge of her phone call.

'Jessica…' he murmured, his rich accented drawl rather flat in tone and delivery, brilliant dark eyes shrewd and distinctly wary.

'I guess the phrase, "Fancy seeing you here" really belongs to me!' Jess quipped loudly, determined not to show her distress either through tears or temper. 'After all, I was still under the impression that you were working eighteen hour days in Milan!'

Cesario surveyed her levelly. 'I'm sorry that I lied to you—'

'But why did you lie? That's what I want to know.'

'I don't think you *will* want to know once I explain,' Cesario countered. 'And that's the main reason why I kept you out of the situation.'

Refusing to engage with that baffling forecast and assurance, Jess snatched in a steadying breath and then asked bluntly, 'Were you ever in Milan?'

'No. I've been in London throughout the week.'

'With Alice?' she prompted jerkily.

Cesario regarded her with frowning force

and a tangible air of bewilderment. 'Why would Alice be here?'

'I thought perhaps you were having an affair with her,' Jess advanced rather reluctantly, because it was so patently obvious from his pained expression that sexual shenanigans with his cousin's wife had played no part in his pretence about his whereabouts.

'No,' he proclaimed in blunt dissent. 'You thought wrong.'

'Maybe not with Alice, but possibly with someone else?' Jess persisted, unable to quite let go of her suspicions regarding his fidelity.

'*Dio mio*, sex with anyone other than you has to be the last thing on my mind right now,' Cesario responded with an impatience that dispelled her concerns in that field better than any heated denial would have done.

'Well, I don't know what goes on in your mind, do I?' In reaction to the sudden release of her tension, because the spectre of Alice and that past affair had loomed like a very large threat in her mind, Jess threw up her hands in an unusually dramatic gesture and stalked over to the window. Ebony curls danced on her slim shoulders as she swivelled back to look at him, her profile taut and pale.

'You told me you were in Milan and you were lying!' she reminded him fiercely.

'I have to confess that since we met I have kept a lot from you, *piccola mia*,' Cesario declared.

'Stop hinting and start telling!' Jess flung in direct challenge, angry grey eyes bright as silver stars above her flushed cheekbones.

'I really thought we could do this without anyone getting hurt,' Cesario breathed in a raw undertone. 'But with hindsight I can see now that I was depressed when I asked you to marry me. I was looking for a way out and a means of distraction—'

'Just get to the point, Cesario!' Jess cut in furiously, wondering what on earth he could have been depressed about, while bristling at the suggestion that marrying her had been a means of distraction. That made her sound insultingly like an entertainment act he had hired for his amusement.

'Eight months ago, I had a series of medical tests and, with the diagnosis, life as I knew it came to a sudden end,' Cesario revealed in a driven undertone, his strong facial bones taut beneath his bronzed skin. 'I had been suffering from intermittent problems with my balance and vision and also severe headaches. A scan revealed that I had a brain tumour.'

Totally unprepared for the startling turn that the dialogue had taken, Jess simply stared at him and parroted weakly, 'A brain tumour?'

'Although the tumour is benign, I learned that surgery could leave me seriously disabled and that was a risk I was not prepared to take. I decided that I valued the quality of the life I had left more than the quantity, and I refused further treatment,' Cesario revealed quietly.

Shock had drained the blood from Jess's face and made her tummy flip a somersault. She was struggling to absorb what he had told her and it was so far removed from what she had expected that she was utterly stunned. 'Your migraines…your fall last week…'

'Caused by the tumour,' he confirmed, his jaw line clenching at the reminder. 'My condition has been worsening faster than I had expected and becoming unpredictable, which is why I came to London to undergo more tests this past week—'

'You're telling me that you knew you were *dying* when you asked me to marry you,' Jess almost whispered as she finally put that scenario together for her own benefit and reeled from the ramifications of it. 'When you asked me to have a baby with you, you must have known that you wouldn't be here for that child while it was growing up. How could you deceive me like that?'

Beneath her hail of accusing words, Cesario had lost colour. 'I only appreciated how selfish I was being last week when you told me that you had conceived...'

'Selfish and irresponsible!' Jess slammed back loudly at him, outraged and bitterly hurt that he could have kept her in ignorance of such a crucial if unpalatable fact from the outset of their relationship. 'I knew you weren't planning to stay married to me for ever, but I did believe that you would be available to act as father to our child...you allowed me to believe that!'

In addition, Jess was already working out that while Cesario had kept secrets from her she had been in a minority. Clearly Stefano and Alice had known that Cesario had a brain tumour. Now she understood the often anxious looks she had seen Stefano angling at his cousin. Now she knew exactly what Alice had been getting at when Jess had overheard the other woman arguing with Cesario. Alice, bless her heart, had been trying to persuade

Cesario that day that he ought to tell his wife about his condition, Jess registered belatedly. Of course, she was fairly sure that Alice had no idea that Cesario's was a marriage of convenience built on practicality rather than love and trust. And Cesario's revelations had just blown Jess and all her misconceptions about him and their relationship right out of the water and left her floundering in alien territory.

'Tell me everything,' Jess urged grittily.

'It was not a complete lie when I said I needed a child to inherit Collina Verde,' Cesario continued grimly. 'My grandfather did leave a complex will and to inherit I did have to name Stefano and his son as my heirs because I didn't have a child of my own. But I used that inheritance claim as an excuse when all I really wanted was a child to leave my wealth to—without a child, everything I had worked for all my life suddenly seemed so shallow and pointless.'

And with a shrug of a broad shoulder on that grudging admission, Cesario half turned away from her. He spread expressive lean brown hands in a gesture of frustration that appealed for her understanding. 'I thought I was seeing clearly, but my rationale was warped and short-sighted. I believed I was doing something good, something worthwhile...'

'How could it possibly have been worthwhile?' Jess couldn't think straight. She had come to London to find out where she stood with the man she loved and he had thrown everything she thought she knew about him and their marriage on its head. Her heart thudding fast behind her breastbone, she studied him in growing disbelief as he unwound the tangle of falsehoods he had spread to lay the truth bare for her.

'I saw a child as a worthwhile investment for the future I didn't have,' Cesario extended heavily. 'But I was kidding myself—I was really only thinking about what *I* wanted, not about what truly mattered. And I wanted you from the first moment I saw you.'

But Jess was not prepared to listen to that line of argument. In concert with what he was telling her, she felt as though her own life were shattering and falling down around her in broken irreparable pieces. Nothing was as she had thought, nothing was as it had seemed. The fabulous honeymoon in Italy had been a mere passage out of time—*a means of distraction*—and essentially meaningless. Cesario had cruelly deceived her from the start. He wasn't going to be there for her as a husband, or as a father for their child, or even as a former partner in another country, she registered sickly. He wasn't going to be there for her at all.

'Everything you told me was a lie,' she began in condemnation.

'And honesty is very important to you...I know,' Cesario returned with a sardonic edge to his voice. 'I'm not trying to minimise the effect of what I did to you. It was wrong.'

Jess settled embittered eyes on him. 'But it's too late for regret now. I'm married to you and pregnant!'

Cesario stared at her with deep, dark bronzed eyes and it was as if she was seeing him clearly for the first time. He was so handsome and so sexy, but he was also unfathomable, with depths that she had not even come close to plumbing, she acknowledged unhappily, feeling her ignorance bite to the very foot of her soul.

'We can separate right now if you like. It's not a problem,' Cesario informed her quietly. 'I'm prepared for that.'

Jess flinched as if he had jabbed a red-hot branding iron near bare skin. She wanted to shout and scream back at him like a fishwife in response to that offhand statement, which set such a low and casual value on their marriage. It was a direct reminder of the practical agreement on which their union was based. Only fierce pride kept the tide of her rising emotions taped down and under control. He was offering her her freedom back as though their marriage had indeed only been a temporary diversion for a man whose future would be taken from him when he least expected it. He was showing her the door. He was politely letting her know that, although he had lied to her and kept her in the dark, it didn't ultimately matter because he didn't care enough even to try to hang onto her.

'The baby,' she mumbled sickly.

'I'm sorry, I'm very sorry that I got you involved in this,' Cesario muttered roughly. 'I know that's not good enough but, apart from money, it's all I've got to give you right now.'

Jess lifted what shreds of dignity remained to her and dealt him a scornful smile of dismissal. 'I don't need your money!'

'I'm signing the Halston Hall estate over to you this week.'

Jess was trembling; appalled by the way he was concentrating on financial arrangements for their separation when her heart was breaking up inside her and her sense of loss was dragging her down so deep and so fast she felt as if she were drowning. 'Oh, goody, I'll own the Dunn-Montgomery ancestral home—how fitting!' she exclaimed with a brittle laugh, desperate to hide her pain and spinning around in an unchoreographed half circle to conceal her emotion from his keen appraisal.

'What are you talking about?'

'I never got around to telling you but I'm actually an illegitimate Dunn-Montgomery,' Jess told him in an artificially bright voice. 'Robert Martin married my mother when I was ten months old but I wasn't his child. My father is the member of parliament, William Dunn-Montgomery, although he will never admit the fact. He was a student when he got my mother pregnant—'

'And that's why Luke was so taken with you at our wedding—he knows he's your half-brother!' Cesario guessed, frowning at her in sudden comprehension as he made that familial connection. '*Madre di Dio!* Is that why you married me? To get Halston Hall?'

Thunderstruck by that suggestion, Jess stared blankly back at him.

'I can see that my ownership of the house would have been a major attraction to someone in your circumstances,' Cesario said drily.

Jess had turned pale. 'Someone in my circumstances?'

'You said yourself how fitting it would be that you should own the former ancestral home of the Dunn-Montgomerys, when your birth father refuses to even acknowledge your relationship,' Cesario extended. 'I don't mind. In fact it's a relief if Halston Hall can in some way compensate you for the way in which I've screwed up your life.'

There was a note of finality to that assurance. His dark golden eyes were cool, his stubborn sensual mouth composed in a firm line. For the first time since her arrival she knew exactly what he was thinking: he had said all he had to say to her and now he was ready for her to leave. For several seconds she withstood the steady onslaught of his gaze, because a crushing sense of rejection was holding her in a near state of paralysis, and then she moved away on feet that felt as if they didn't belong to the rest of her body.

Cesario was making a phone call in his own language but both his voice and actions seemed to be happening far away at the end of a long dark tunnel. Jess felt detached from her surroundings and horribly light-headed.

'You'll be driven home…no, don't argue with me,' Cesario urged as her lips parted. 'You're pregnant. I don't want you struggling to find a seat on a packed train during the rush hour.'

With enormous effort, Jess focused on him. She dimly recognised that she was in a state of shock so profound that she could barely think, but there was one question that she could not suppress. 'You said your condition had got worse…how long?' and her voice ran out of steam altogether and just vanished in the awfulness of what she was saying.

'They're not quite sure. Not more than six months,' he proffered with unnatural calm. 'I do have one favour to ask…'

'What?' Jess prompted shakily, for the number six was whizzing round and round inside her head as if someone had turned on a manic mixer.

'Would you mind if Weed and Magic lived with me? For as long as that's practical,' Cesario extended tight-mouthed.

Jess felt as if someone had their hands squeezing round her throat: it was that hard to breathe and there was a pain building in her chest. She was recalling the patient way he had learned hand signals so that he could communicate with the deaf terrier. 'No problem,' she said, schooling her voice to control it. 'No problem at all.'

Rigo Castello escorted her in silence down to the basement car park and tucked her into a limousine. She remembered the older man's behaviour when Cesario had collapsed and realised that he had been in on the secret as well. It seemed that of all the people close to Cesario she had been just about the only one kept in the dark. Deceived, lied to, shut out of the charmed circle and, although he wanted her dogs for company, he didn't want her…

# CHAPTER TEN

THE instant Jess laid eyes on her mother that evening she started to cry. Once she had let that flood of pent-up grief and despair flow freely there was no stopping it.

Shaken by the state her daughter was in, Sharon Martin took some time to grasp the situation that her daughter was describing between heartbroken sobs. When Jess had finally mopped her eyes dry, her eyelids were so swollen she could hardly see out of them. But she had only to think of Cesario and more moisture trickled down her quivering cheeks.

'You're the first person in my family ever to go to university and yet when it comes to a real crisis you act as if you're as thick as two short planks!' Sharon pronounced, shocking her daughter right out of her self-preoccupied silence.

'How can you say that?' Jess gasped.

'The man you say you love is dying and you're still whinging on about how he lied to you! What are you thinking of?' the older woman demanded.

*The man you love is dying.* And there it was, the simple fact that had frozen Jess's ability to reason at source. That news had torn her apart, both angering and terrifying her, for she did not know how to handle something so enormous and threatening that it affected her entire world and destroyed even the future.

'Cesario lied to protect you and, by the looks of it, he knew what he was doing when he lied, because you're sitting here being useless!' Sharon scolded. 'Where is your brain, Jess? He doesn't want you to feel that you *have* to stay with him because you're his wife and he's ill. He knows you didn't sign up for that and he clearly never intended to tell you. Obviously he thought he was going to have more time with you. He doesn't want your pity. That's why he told you that you could have a separation right now, so that you are free to do whatever *you* like.'

Blinking rapidly, Jess stared back at her mother. 'What *I* like?' she echoed.

'A week ago you were in Italy with Cesario

and you were both very, very happy, weren't you?' Sharon voiced that reminder gently.

'Yes, but—'

'No buts. Cesario can't have changed that much in the space of a few days. He's just giving you the chance to escape getting involved in his illness.'

'You honestly believe he's trying to protect me rather than get rid of me?' Jess whispered shakily.

'I think that's the only reason he lied all along. He's trying to be a tough guy and deal with his condition alone.'

Jess swallowed the thickness in her throat and stared down at her feet with glazed eyes. 'I don't think I can handle losing him,' she framed gruffly.

'Then don't give up. By the sound of it, he's already given up, so he doesn't need more of the same from you. There may still be room for hope. You tell him he has to give the treatment a go—for your sake and the baby's,' the older woman proffered briskly. 'With any luck, it won't be too late for him to change his mind.'

Jess grasped that thought like a mental lifeline and held fast to it. 'I've been stupid, blind, self-obsessed…'

'You were in shock and now you've had the chance to think things through. You have to fight for most things in life that are worth having.'

'I'll go back to London…'

'Tomorrow. Right now you're exhausted and you need a good night's sleep before you do anything,' Sharon told her firmly. 'You have to look after yourself and the baby now.'

The next morning Jess had a routine surgery to carry out and it was the afternoon before she had the leisure to think. A deep longing for Cesario's presence clawed at her, filling her with fear of the future all over again, but also hardening her resolve to take action. She drove back to the hall, gazing out at the gracious old house, and while marvelling that it was now her home she frowned at the sight of the pair of vans already parked outside.

It was an unpleasant surprise to walk into the big hall and see a stack of boxes piled up. Looking beyond them, she could see the amount of activity going on in Cesario's office, people moving about busily while desk and cupboards were cleared and packed. Her heart sank to the soles of her feet and she felt sick: he was already moving out!

Without any warning, Cesario appeared in the doorway, Weed and Magic at his heels. That he looked so healthy with his vibrant golden skin tone hit her like a slap in the face, while the cloaked and unrevealing darkness of his gaze simply hurt her. Once again she felt excluded, on the outside when she wanted to be involved in everything he did.

He strolled fluidly closer, as elegant as he always was in a pearl grey business suit, only the absence of a tie striking a less formal note. He looked gorgeous. In spite of the pain Jess was fighting to hold at bay, her heart started to pound very, very fast inside her.

'I'm sorry—this isn't how I planned this. I intended to be gone before you got back from work,' he admitted levelly.

'It won't do you any good,' Jess told him tartly. 'I'll just follow you to London and camp out on your doorstep.'

His brow indented and he gave her a bemused look. 'I'm sorry?'

'I want to be with you. I *need* to be with you,' Jess said boldly. 'Blame yourself for that. You dragged me into this.'

'We'll talk in the drawing room,' he breathed tautly, lush ebony lashes lowering to screen his gaze from the intrusion of hers.

'Nothing you could possibly say will change my mind,' Jess warned him, lifting her chin as he closed the door on the hall and the bustle of the packers.

'You're taking an emotional view of this situation and that's wrong.'

'Maybe it would be wrong for you, but it's not wrong for me,' Jess cut in with assurance.

'You're thinking of me the way you think of your rescue animals—all starry-eyed compassion and do-gooding instincts to the fore,' he condemned, his lean, strong face rigid with censure. 'I don't want that. I can't live with that.'

'And I can't live with you dealing with this alone and away from me, so it seems that we're at an impasse,' Jess pronounced, taking in the disorientated look starting to build in his beautiful dark golden eyes and the anger that she was behaving in a way he had not foreseen. 'We're also about to have a major argument.'

A black brow lifted. 'About what?' he challenged, an aggressive angle to his strong jaw.

'You have to go for that treatment you refused—'

'No.' The rebuttal was instant.

'Stop thinking about you and think about this baby you decided to bring into this world.' Jess shot that fiery advice back at him without hesitation. 'Our baby deserves that you fight this by any means open to you. If there's the smallest chance that you can survive this, you *owe* it to us to take it!'

Cesario gazed back at her with unflinching force but he had lost colour. 'Strong words…'

'Strongly felt,' Jess traded, holding that look with intent grey eyes that willed him to listen, for she felt as if she was fighting for both their lives. When the tumour had first been diagnosed he had taken a stance and, in her opinion, he had taken the wrong one.

'And what of the consequences if the surgery doesn't go well?'

Jess squared her slim shoulders. 'Then we'll deal with that when and if it happens. We'll manage. You're luckier than most people in that you can afford the best medical care and support if you need it.'

'But what if I'm not prepared to live with the risk of being maimed?' Cesario pressed darkly.

'Life is precious, Cesario. Life is *very*

precious,' Jess whispered vehemently, longing for him to accept that truth. 'I can tell
you now that our child would rather have you
alive and disabled than not have you at all.'

'I'm not going to ask you how you feel!'
Cesario shot back at her in a derisive attack
that cut a painful swathe through her anxiety.
'I'm talking to a woman with a three-legged,
half-blind dog and a deaf dog and several
others with what you might term a "reduced
quality of life", so I already know your liberal
views. But I'm not a dumb animal and my
needs are a little more sophisticated!'

'But you are also putting your pride and
need to be independent ahead of every other
factor and you're assuming that the worst case
scenario will result,' Jess condemned in a
determined attack on his outlook. 'Why so
pessimistic? What happened to hope? What's
wrong with having hope? We have a child on
the way. I'm asking you to think about what
having a father will mean to our baby as he
or she grows up.'

Cesario compressed his lips. 'I'm not the
right person to discuss that with because I had
a rotten father.'

'All the more reason for you to think this
over now, because you could do the job better.

I had a rotten birth father as well. He gave my mother the money for an abortion and considered his responsibility to us both concluded. But Robert Martin was a wonderful father to me,' Jess declared with passionate sincerity. 'He's not educated and he's not clever or successful like my birth father, but I love him very much for always being there to love, support and encourage me. What's in your heart is what matters, not the superficial things.'

'You were fortunate.'

Her face took on a wry expression. 'But sadly I didn't appreciate just how lucky I was to have Robert, until William Dunn-Montgomery had a solicitor's letter sent to me warning me to stay away from him and his family.'

Cesario frowned, taken aback by that admission. 'When did that happen?'

'When I was a student of nineteen and I tried to meet my birth father. It was after I got out of hospital following the stalker attack. I was going through a difficult time emotionally and I was madly curious about my beginnings and rather naïve in my expectations. Sadly, William Dunn-Montgomery took fright at my first approach and made it very clear that he wanted nothing to do with me,' she explained with a grimace. 'It took that experience of rejection for me to realise how privileged I'd been to have a stepfather like Robert, who always treated me as a daughter he was proud of.'

'I can understand the depth of your loyalty to him now,' Cesario conceded heavily. 'I wish I hadn't taken advantage of it.'

'Never mind that now. Having a father enriched my life. All I'm asking is that you try to give our child the same advantage.'

Dark eyes bleak and without a shade of gold, Cesario breathed curtly, 'I'll bear that in mind, but I have thought long and hard about this and I have already made my decision.'

Jess released her breath in a slow hiss, the ferocious tension holding her taut draining out of her again to leave her feeling limp and wrung out. 'Decisions can be changed!' she argued.

'But that decision was made six months ago. Surgery may not even be an option any more.'

That risk hadn't really occurred to Jess. Up until that point all she had focused on was getting him to change his mind and consider treatment. Now all she could think about was how cruel it would be if Cesario was destined to die because he had met her too late.

Cesario searched her distraught face. 'You and that baby have me over a barrel.'

'That's not how I want you to feel.'

'I'm meeting with my doctors tomorrow—'

Her eyes widened fearfully. 'I'm coming too. From now on, you don't shut me out any more.'

'This was supposed to be a practical marriage. I never wanted you to get involved in this!' Cesario derided in a sudden burst of very masculine frustration.

'I decide what I want to get involved in,' Jess responded squarely.

'You'll regret it,' he told her grimly. 'At any time, feel free to walk away from this and me.'

'I'm not going anywhere,' Jess informed him stubbornly. 'And, by the way, I didn't marry you to gain the right to live in this house because it once belonged to the Dunn-Montgomery family. Nor did I marry you purely to save my stepfather's skin. I also wanted a child of my own—you and I had the same agenda.'

His lush lashes cloaked his gaze and the

lean hands he had coiled into fists loosened again. He released his breath on a sigh. 'I know that, but it doesn't alter the fact that I used your stepfather's plight to put you under unfair pressure to marry me.'

'That's not how you felt about it at the time,' Jess reminded him. 'And if we're staying together, please tell your staff to put the office contents back.'

A faint touch of colour edging his high cheekbones, Cesario went to speak to his staff and the moving operation went into sudden reverse. Jess started to breathe a little easier when the first box went back through the office doorway instead of out of the house.

Taking off his jacket, Cesario strode back to her side, beautiful dark eyes lustrous, rousing a tiny scream of pain and fear inside her. How could he look so well and yet be so very far from well? Suppressing that negative thought, she sensed his uncertainty and she reached for his hand in an instinctive gesture of unity.

'Let's go upstairs where we'll get some peace,' he urged in the midst of the bustle around them, and he directed her towards the magnificent staircase.

'There are things I have to say to you, *mia bella*,' Cesario said very seriously before they reached the bedroom they invariably shared. 'Things that I wanted to say weeks ago in Italy but which I felt then were better left unspoken.'

'So, get them out of the way now,' Jess urged, wondering in some apprehension what he had held back from saying to her. 'We shouldn't have any more secrets from each other.'

Cesario studied her intently. 'I blackmailed you into marrying me, *moglie mia*,' he intoned with regret. 'I wanted you and I didn't care how I got you. But no matter how you feel about it now, it was incredibly selfish of me to plunge you into this situation.'

'You'd be surprised how resilient I am.' Jess lifted her head high, her grey gaze soft and strong as it rested on him. 'And, yes, you blackmailed me, but I was attracted to you as well and without the pressure you put on me I would never have done anything about it. Never mind what happens in the future; I'll always be glad we did get together,' she completed gruffly.

'But I feel like I've trapped you now. You're way too nice to put yourself first and walk away from a dying partner,' Cesario derided in a frustrated undertone.

'You may not die. You *must* look at the more positive angle,' Jess breathed feelingly. 'And I'm not too nice. If I didn't want to be with you, I wouldn't be here now because I couldn't fake it, I couldn't pretend...'

He touched her damp cheek with a gentle forefinger and looked down into her open gaze. 'No. I don't think you could fake what you feel either and it's one of the things that I love most about you. What you see is what you get, but I'm still taking advantage of your good nature and loyalty—'

Jess was so tense that she might as well have been poised on a cliff edge. 'Did you just say that you loved me?'

'I am hopelessly in love with you—didn't you guess?' Cesario vented a rueful laugh. 'I thought I was kind of obvious.'

Jess was trembling. 'I can be a bit slow on the uptake sometimes,' she said shakily. 'When did you realise you felt that way?'

'In Italy when it was a challenge just to be away from you for a couple of hours,' Cesario confided huskily. 'I've never felt like that before.'

'Not even about Alice?' Jess heard herself ask, and then she winced, wishing she had not let that petty jealous question escape her lips.

'Jess, you have never had any reason to worry about the relationship I once had with Alice. I like and respect Alice a great deal but we were a mismatch. When I was with her, I was too young to want to settle down and even though I was unfaithful she never stood up to me.' Cesario shared those uncomfortable truths and grimaced. 'I'm not proud of the way I treated her. I only realised that I did care about her when she was gone from my life. But I never loved her the way Stefano loves her and I wouldn't have married her because my feelings didn't go deep enough for that.'

'I'm sorry to keep on going on about Alice,' Jess said ruefully as she linked her arms round his broad shoulders, her fears about the other woman finally laid to rest by his candour. 'But when I overheard you and Alice talking the night before we left Italy it did make me wary of your friendship with her.'

Cesario frowned. 'What did you overhear?'

And once Jess had explained, he heaved a groan of comprehension. 'Alice and Stefano have known about my condition from the start, and Alice was correct when she said that I wasn't being fair to you in not telling you. But those weeks we shared in Italy were some of the happiest of my life…and I didn't want to sacrifice a day of that to the reality of my condition.'

That declaration made her eyes prickle with tears. But she swiftly blinked the betraying moisture back because she knew he would take the wrong message from it and return to believing that he was the worst thing that had ever happened to her when in fact he was the best. 'I fell in love with you in Italy as well.'

'I was ahead of you there,' Cesario claimed, tipping up her chin with his fingers to look down into her silvery grey eyes. 'I probably fell for you at the moment I saw you in your wedding gown at the church—you looked like my every dream come true. And that's from a guy who never thought he was romantic.'

Jess had never felt that, for a thousand and one little and large romantic gestures had made their honeymoon special. But she smiled up at him with her heart in her eyes. 'I love you so much…'

'I'm never going to stop wanting you, *amata mia*,' Cesario pronounced with driven sincerity, brilliant dark eyes pinned to her with adoring intensity. 'But I didn't want to do this to you. I wanted to make you happy, not sad.'

'And whatever happens you *will* make me happy,' Jess told him with confidence. 'Every day we have together now is a day we wouldn't have had, if you had succeeded in scaring me off yesterday.'

'But it's not fair to put you through this with me,' Cesario groaned, unable to hide his guilty look of concern.

Jess smoothed gentle fingertips across the taut line of one high masculine cheekbone. 'How would you feel if it was me that had the tumour? Could you just walk away?'

'*Infierno!* Are you joking?' Cesario demanded incredulously.

'Well, then, don't expect me to be any different. I love you too,' she reminded him. 'I want to be with you, whatever happens.'

And in a flood of passionate appreciation that he could not hide from her, Cesario covered her mouth with his and kissed her breathless. She trailed his jacket off in the midst of it, embarked on undoing his shirt buttons and spread loving hands over the warmth of his hair-roughened torso. His lean, strong body was urgent and aroused against hers and she shut out the negative thoughts that lurked ready to threaten her happiness.

The man she loved loved her back with the same heat and passion and, for now, that was enough for her. She would take happiness where she could find it and make the most of every moment with him.

Rio, named Cesario at birth after his father, kicked the ball and it hit a window with a loud thump followed by the noise of shattering glass.

*'Mamma!'* he yelled in dismay.

Jess, who had been sitting in the shade of the loggia, rose to her feet and hurried along the terrace to ensure that her son stayed well away from the broken glass while shooing away the dogs at the same time. She checked his clothing for tiny shards, moved him well clear of the debris and then smiled at Tommaso. Having returned the ball, the older man, a long look of calm resignation on his face, was already advancing with a brush and shovel to clear up the mess. It was expected that a lively little boy would practise his football moves and, at five years old, boys didn't come much livelier than Rio.

He was blessed with his father's lustrous

dark eyes and his mother's black curls; his decided appeal made it very likely that some day he would be a heartbreaker as well. Born a week after his due date in a straightforward delivery, Rio had delighted his mother from the first moment he'd drawn breath and motherhood had more than lived up to all her expectations, though been rather more tiring than she had appreciated. Although Rio had been a very good-natured baby he had also required little sleep and after more interrupted nights than she still cared to recall Jess had been glad to have the support of a good nanny. Having inherited his parents' stubborn streak, determination and intelligence, Rio could be a handful.

Her entire family enjoyed a long summer holiday at Collina Verde every year. Her parents were currently attending evening classes in Italian and working hard to learn the language. Her half-brothers still worked on the Halston estate, but her father had surprised them all by finding a new job at a local garden centre where he was happily employed as a deputy manager. Jess was also in regular contact with her other brother, Luke Dunn-Montgomery, and the previous year he and his girlfriend had joined her for a winter break at Cesario's opulent villa in Morocco. She had heard nothing more from her birth father but was content with that situation. Alice and Stefano and their children were regular visitors, and Alice had gradually become Jess's best friend. The couples shared family events and celebrations.

Soon after Rio's birth, Jess had opted to buy into the veterinary practice as a partner and she still worked part-time hours. That same year, her animal sanctuary had won charitable status. Full-time employees, assisted by a rota of volunteers, now kept the rescue facility running efficiently and many animals had been happily rehomed since the sanctuary had reopened on the Halston estate. Dozy, her narcoleptic greyhound, was asleep by the wall next to Johnson, her collie. Harley the Labrador and Hugs the wolfhound had passed away due to old age, but their places had since been filled by Owen, a lively Jack Russell, who acted as a seeing-eye guide to his friend, Bix, a blind Great Dane. Weed and Magic, however, were now scampering cheerfully in the wake of the two little girls running across the terrace.

Graziella, an adorable three-year-old, with her mother's light grey eyes, rushed to show Jess the painting she had done at the summer playgroup she attended. Her little sister, Allegra, an apple-cheeked toddler of eighteen months with an explosion of black curls, bowled along behind Graziella like a shadow.

Jess gathered both girls into her arms with a grin but her whole face lit up when Cesario, her tall, dark and very handsome husband, strode out of the house. He bounced a new football across the terrace to Rio, who gave a whoop of pleasure and grabbed both ball and father in his enthusiasm, chattering in ninety-mile-an-hour Italian about the window he had broken.

'Daddy didn't play music in the car like I wanted,' confided Graziella crossly. 'We had football.'

From beneath the vine-covered loggia, Jess surveyed the man she loved with amused eyes. He made a special effort to take time off and spend it with his family during the long summers they usually spent at Collina Verde. Although she rarely thought back now to the period when she had feared she would lose Cesario, because she felt it was good to move on mentally, she valued the happiness she had found with him and her children all the more from the knowledge that she could so easily have lost him.

Having changed his mind and finally agreed to accept treatment, Cesario had benefited from the latest neurosurgical techniques. Stereotactic surgery, in which CT images were used to pinpoint the location of the tumour and target it with carefully controlled doses of gamma radiation, had been utilised and this non-invasive method had protected all healthy tissue from damage. He had spent only three days in hospital and, after a successful procedure, had experienced neither complications nor subsequent problems. The tumour was gone and follow-up scans remained reassuringly clear.

'Do you think we're spoiling Graziella?' Cesario remarked as their nanny, Izzy, put in an appearance to take the children indoors for lunch. 'She's a real little bossy-boots.'

'I wonder who she gets that from,' Jess commented tongue in cheek, since she had noticed that her elder daughter could twist her father round her little finger with just the suggestion of tears or disappointment. 'Or do you think it could be that maybe she just doesn't like football radio commentaries?'

A wickedly appreciative grin slashed

Cesario's wide sensual mouth. 'She takes after her *mamma* then, her very beautiful, very much loved—'

'And very pregnant *mamma*,' Jess completed, hopelessly conscious of the size of her pregnant body on such a warm day. She was within weeks of her delivery date for their fourth child. She already knew that she was carrying a second boy, who would very probably be christened Roberto after his doting grandfather. Their children had given them both so much joy that they weren't quite sure when they would consider their family complete.

Cesario splayed a protective hand across the proud swell of her belly. 'Very beautiful, very pregnant *mamma*,' he traded huskily as he pulled her back against him, 'whom I was extremely lucky to find and marry in my hour of greatest need.'

Jess leant back against the support of his big powerful body and sighed in blissful relaxation, enjoying a moment of perfect peace without the children providing a distraction. 'We found each other and once I had had a taste of you and Italy I knew you were the man for me. I love you so much.'

Cesario turned her slowly round in the

circle of his arms and looked down into the silvery grey eyes he still found so enthralling. 'The love of my life,' he breathed and kissed her with tender loving care…

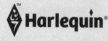

## HARLEQUIN® HISTORICAL
### Where love is timeless

*Imagine a time of chivalrous knights*
*and unconventional ladies,*
*roguish rakes and impetuous heiresses,*
*rugged cowboys and*
*spirited frontierswomen—*
*these rich and vivid tales*
*will capture your imagination!*

## HARLEQUIN HISTORICAL...
## THEY'RE TOO GOOD TO MISS!